THE COMPETITION OF UNFINISHED STORIES

COVER DESIGN Cooley Design Lab
COVER PHOTOGRAPH © Sener Ozmen; The Patient, 2012
DESIGN & LAYOUT Nikša Eršek
PUBLISHED BY Sandorf Passage
South Portland, Maine, United States
IMPRINT OF Sandorf
Severinska 30, Zagreb, Croatia
sandorfpassage.org
PRINTED BY Znanje, Zagreb

Sandorf Passage books are available to the trade through Independent Publishers Group: ipgbook.com | (800) 888-4741.

Library of Congress Control Number: 2025937032

ISBN: 978-9-53351-534-2

Also available as an ebook;
ISBN: 978-9-53351-535-9

THE COMPETITION OF UNFINISHED STORIES

Translated by Nicholas Glastonbury

Sener Ozmen

SAN-
DORF
PAS-
SAGE

SOUTH PORTLAND | MAINE

For *Arab Shamilov*, father of the Kurdish novel,
And for my son, *Robîn* . . .

“Ehmeq in yên di xeletiyên xwe de bi israr in.”

“Fools are those who persist in their mistakes.”

SEYÎD EVDILHEKÎMÊ ARWASÎ

Preface

THE FIRST TIME I saw him was in October 1998, in the house in Mêrsîn that I'd shared with my older sister, Yasemîn, for three and a half years. He sat in the kitchen of that house, which had two narrow rooms and an exceedingly large den; he sat facing Yasemîn, sipping on his cooling Nescafé and explaining something to her in that low-pitched voice of his. I was struck not by what he was saying about Marxism—I couldn't care less—but by the tone of his voice. His charming, altogether masculine voice resonated in the kitchen that Friday morning, and after Onder's *shrill* and *agonized* sniveling, which had pushed a girl like me to the edge, it seemed like an unexpected sign from above.

Fourteen days after our first encounter, I saw him for the second time, the person to whom that voice belonged—I mean *Sertac* (we had our first argument that night, which broke out because I mispronounced his name; it's supposed to be *Sertac*, a hard "dj" sound, not *Sertaç* with a "ch." As far as he was concerned, there was a mortal difference between "c" and "ç" that I couldn't possibly understand, and, anyway, he had pulled out his ID right away to prove it to me, telling me how his father had argued with the birth clerk about that single dumb letter; if you ask me, he really didn't need to go into so much detail), I mean, *Sertac Karan*—in my room, to put it politely, in my bed. He had slipped out of the kitchen and out of Yasemîn's heart, in that order, and toddled his way to me. I had become the one who'd stolen him from Yasemîn, yes, me, from my sister! But he had ended up with me, lock, stock, and barrel; he was naked and seemed ashamed of his nakedness, and I was stroking his deflated lighthouse with my lust-hungry fingertips. That night, in the light of the fourteen candles I'd placed around my room, Sertac fell asleep, long before me, or my sister in the kitchen. His sleep was as magnetic as his voice.

* * *

It was a rainy day, and I had finished my Contemporary Turkish Literature makeup exam quite early. I screwed myself over by rushing through so many of the questions, and so I made a beeline to Onder.

When I arrived at the hallowed door of his hallowed office, I knocked gently, as was my custom, and he replied, "Come in!" in his half-dead voice, as was his custom. I hated this meaningless and unnecessary ceremony!* Like most things I did out of

* Setting aside the fact that Merasîm's name literally means "ceremony" in Kurdish, who among us has not abased themselves for a chance at the right romance with the wrong person (or the wrong romance with the right person)? (Trans.)

obligation, knocking on the door had quickly become another ritual cornerstone of our relationship, thoroughly enclosed by new sets of rules on every last goddamned day of the Lord.

Onder had warned me of this in the first days of our relationship. Picture it: We were in his office, sitting opposite each other with his *demirbaş*[*] desk between us; "This isn't something to take lightly!" he said, a sour look on his face.

"No, Merasîm, no," he continued with an academic air, tapping the butt of his ballpoint pen on the desk over and over. "It's wrong for you to barge into my office! I'm the teacher, you're my student, this is a house of knowledge; plus, you know I don't want to draw the attention of my colleagues. Whenever you want to see me, please just call me first and . . ." And, and what? No, no way, I couldn't make any sense of what he was saying. Because the night before, this very same Onder had asked me, begged me, in fact, to do the most jaw-dropping, unspeakable things. I felt nauseous, and yet I couldn't bring myself to tell him no.

"You see, that's how men are," my sister said later. "Quit playing dumb! The history of men, history in the broadest sense, has shown to us oppressed women—and let me underscore the word *oppressed*—that when it comes to sex, the dumbest of men, the craziest of men, and even, even, even the

* *Demirbaş*: a Turkish word *literally* meaning "ironhead," it most often refers to a standard-issue object or piece of official or state property, something both necessary to and taken for granted within a place, like an ugly bureaucrat in a government office, or a couch and a pile of magazines in a psychiatrist's waiting room, or a soldier with a machine gun standing at the ready on any and every street corner. (Trans.)

smartest of men, your Onder falls into this category, they all fall into the same hole . . ." Yasemîn went on like this, making sure to land a few choice barbs about my relationship with Onder, which she'd always looked down on. And so, the main topic of our daily conversations soon became Onder, my *academic* man; it became almost impossible to talk about anything else at home, and Yasemîn absolutely wore me down with her unending questions. I had to accept that my sister was weird about it. "You know, you're Onder's *demirbaş*," she blurted out one day. Where she found such phrases I have no idea, but she was right; my sister had summed up our relationship in a single sentence. I think that's exactly how it was: I was "academic" Onder's *demirbaş*, just as Onder was surely a *demirbaş* for others.

* * *

It had become tradition that after we had sex, every single time, he would grab his clothes, dress quickly, and, as soon as he grabbed his backpack, make his way home at some hour of the night. I tried to entice him to spend the night with me, so that he wouldn't run from paradise right after his pitiful wails and moans, so that he wouldn't leave my body alone with my soul. He never did. I don't quite know what his justification was. I attributed these sudden flights to the fact that Yasemîn was at home and he felt uncomfortable with her presence and didn't want to come face-to-face with her after so much hue and cry. I'd considered him to be a *demirbaş* in our house, but I guess he wasn't.

"I think you forget I have a home of my own, and I can't just do whatever I want in someone else's home . . ."

"No, no, no. I have a shower at my house, plus we don't have a water quota." I pointed at the bathroom, telling him he could wash up if he wished, but I remember his expression like it was yesterday, the way he stared daggers at me like I'd issued some impossible demand. I said to him, okay, okay, all I wanted was permission to stay with him from time to time, but he dug in his heels. Had I gone to his house simply for my own pleasure? Yasemîn would go to Stenbol once every two months for seminars and be gone for days at a time. When that happened, I would go to my dear Onder's house at the first opportunity, so I wouldn't be alone, or, more to the point, so I could share my loneliness with him. Things were fine at first; we would cook and eat together, tidy up, toss his dirty clothes in the washer, and find ourselves at the bottom of a wine bottle, listening to eccentric music in a state of mild inebriation. By then it would be his sex hour, I'm not kidding, he'd look at his watch, grab me by the wrist, and pull me into his bedroom, and there my dear Onder would turn into a ball of fire, descending on me. After I gave him some relief, by which I mean after my dear Onder had gotten himself off—it never took too long—we would return to the pace of things, when, as we'd say, "everything was normal." Onder the *academic* would get up and go back to his writing, as though I weren't there, as though we weren't in the same house. In short, what he wanted was for me to get myself together and leave, to get away from there, from him.

"So that's how Onder treats you? And you're still with him? You have no idea what I'd do if I were in your shoes," Yasemîn said, purely out of her own morbid curiosity about what I did or didn't do with Onder, trying to take the words out of my mouth, going on and on and on about his athleticism and his taut body, cracking herself up as she asked demeaning and yet gradually more inquisitive questions about how his muscles quivered in the throes of orgasm.

* * *

Once, and only once, on a whim, I asked Onder for a loan. If only the Earth had split open and swallowed me whole instead. I was filled with a thousand regrets before I even finished the sentence, but by then the train had already left the station. My dad was a little tight that month. The money he'd sent me hadn't even been enough to buy my books. Not to mention my sister was already keeping an account of every last bite of food I ate. He handed me a *demirbaş* envelope of money and said, "Take this. Like you said, it's a loan. Once you finish school and start work, as soon as you get your first paycheck . . ." My jaw was on the floor. I took the envelope and, without another word, fled from his room like a ghost in the night.

* * *

Maybe it was too early for these kinds of things, or else maybe I was being covetous when it came to love, but I was making a lot of demands at once—hitting the town, walking along the water, holding hands, trying to coax genuine words of love out of him, discussing the future of our relationship—but none of those demands seemed possible. Maybe I'd made a mistake from the beginning by embarking on a relationship like this. Onder was too busy fretting over the trials and tribulations of getting tenure. He was burning the candle at both ends, trying to improve his English, flying through dictionaries, taking virtual courses on CDs, muttering to himself, but for one reason or another he simply couldn't make any headway. His method of working was weird too; he'd bought colored Post-it notes, writing words and phrases in English on each of them and sticking them all over his house. It got so bad that I started fearing he was going to stick his notes all over my body.

Eventually, it seemed to me that our relationship had run its course, that we'd basically broken up already. Our romance, which had begun in his office on a beautiful spring day two years earlier, was now on its deathbed, crying its death rattle. We were both aware of that fact, but neither of us could muster up the courage to say so.

* * *

Obviously, of course, he was surrounded by girls who were prettier and more kempt than me, all of them students; they'd stream in and out of his office, trying to be close to him, leaning over his desk and showing him God knows what, giggling the whole time, and why wouldn't they? All those girls with their asses out, competing with one another for a chance to see the body he'd sculpted through exercise, to feel up his shapely muscles; it's not like they wanted to learn anything about literature, to ask him to teach them about writers they didn't know.

Once upon a time, he told me, he had trained as a wrestler, which meant he had spent years at university thoroughly exhausting himself with dumbbells and barbells. He'd grab me and lift me up like I was a barbell, my feet leaving the floor; being up in the air like that made me freak out, and he'd laugh at me, wanting only to show off his strength and his bulging muscles. He was so sure of his strength. But his voice, sickly, simpering, completely at odds with his body, niggled at the ear like a parasite in my skull; it made a mockery of his muscles and slowly soured me to him altogether.

We broke up without a fuss, without fighting or arguing. No beating around the bush.

"It's over," I said.

He was ready for it too. "Suit yourself."

Those snotty girls thronged into his office with their acrid perfumes, preventing me from really sticking it to him, from telling him just how grating I found his voice. They greeted me with their wholly insincere hellos as they filed in and surrounded Onder, who couldn't bring himself to look me in the face. I left his office and went right to the bus stop, rode to the city center, and beelined it to my hairdresser, Cemal.

"I want it so short I can't even grab it with my fingers . . ." Yasemîn called while I was there.

"Are you at school?"

"Uh-uh, I'm at the hairdresser."

"The hairdresser?"

"Uh-huh."

"Why?"

"I decided to cut off all my hair."

"No, really? Well, anyway, I have someone over. Please don't tell me you're coming home early."

"Okay. I was going to go to the movies."

"You good?"

"I'm good, yeah."

* * *

I wanted to leave my sister with her guest—she must have finally found someone—but I didn't want to be alone, so around eight I called home to say I was going to Bensu's place in the Police Quarter to pour my heart out to her. By now my head had shrunk considerably in size, thanks to Cemal shearing away with his scissors, but I still had a skull-splitting headache. I hadn't eaten anything except for a few cookies since morning, and I'd chain-smoked as many cigarettes as there were hairs left on my head. Pîra NAH* had come out of nowhere and landed on my left

* Once upon a time, there was a she-demon named Pîra Mirovxwar, the Man-Eating Witch. Old as time itself, ancient as Lilith, Pîra Mirovxwar has the feet of the bird-monster Anzû and the face of a lion. She drinks the blood of men, devours the menstrual blood of women, and steals away children to cook in her dread furnace. The specter of Pîra Mirovxwar has for millennia been a favorite means of admonishing the naughtiness of children.

But one day—not so long ago, in fact—the howling thaumaturge was astonished to find that the whole of human civilization had managed to far outpace her in the skilled art of cruelty. No longer did parents scare their children into obedience with the very thought of her, for now there were soldiers, guns, and armies to do that job. In this midlife crisis of conscience, brought on by the very fact of modernity, Pîra Mirovxwar took pity on her latest quarry, a beautiful girl-child not yet forty days old, shoulder, chirping like a parrot over and over into my ear, "Suit yourself... Suit yourself... Suit yourself," no matter how many times I tried to swat her away, to keep her from following me all the way to the bus stop. I glanced to my right. One of the posters on the bus stop was for the Ataturkist Thought Association. Among the list of panelists, I saw Onder's photograph—yes, him! My eyes landed not on his face but on the short-sleeved blue shirt I'd given him as a gift in early August. Out of the dozens of gifts I gave him, that was the only one he liked, and he honored me at the time with a single kiss to express his gratitude.

We were at my house.

In the room where I gave up my girlhood to him.

What an unfortunate night.

What a shitty night.

And what a fool you were, Onder.

What an embarrassment!

The heat had driven me out of my mind. We were drenched in sweat from trying to do the very thing we had talked about and decided to do. Onder's doggone yearning, fiery as it was, had burned up eighty percent of the air in the room, leaving both of us panting for the few breaths of oxygen left to us. We

---

and so not yet given a name. Rather than bake and eat this fresh flesh, Pîra Mirovxwar brought the girl to her breast and nursed the baby on her own deathly milk; in so doing, Pîra Mirovxwar made the girl into her daughter, Pîra NAH, the NO-Witch, so named for the resemblance her teeth bore to the beautifully cruel piranha fish in the Amazon River. As she grew, Pîra NAH became a screech-owl sentry for her mother, a nosy naysayer as capriciously mischievous as she was insatiably horny.

This story I know because Pîra NAH told it to me in a dream. (Trans.)

were trying but it just wasn't working. On our third try, Onder suggested that I drink a beer to get over my fear, open up for him without clenching my legs. He put a Dramamine in the glass to heighten the alcohol's effect. Even though I wasn't comfortable with any of this, I took the beer and drank it all. No, alas, it didn't do anything. I didn't feel nauseous, nor did I feel at ease with the plan. Onder stood there bare naked, staring intently at my face, seeing how I might react. His flaccid manhood caught my eye, and when I imagined the scene from the outside I burst out laughing.

And so, his pride injured, *Onder the Sultan* grabbed his clothes off the chair, spitting and hissing as he tried to get dressed. I stopped him. I didn't want him to leave my room empty-handed. I felt like Pîra NAH was there somewhere; my nose burned with her disgusting smell. She must've been in some corner of the room, grumbling as she watched our strange movements. Onder didn't believe he'd done the deed until he saw the blood between my legs with his own eyes. He was all smiles as he got dressed with the boastful air of a man who'd carried out his duty. Me, though, I was laid out on the battlefield, silent, still, defeated, disappointed. I felt so off, like someone had stuck scissors into my crotch and snipped at my vagina, which was *drip-drip-dripping* blood.

Finally, the minibus that would take me to Bensu's arrived, and I got on alongside four men. I sat down next to some old guy, and we were off right away. Nobody but the wide-eyed, dark-skinned, lanky kid stared at my miniskirt. I was well and truly out of it, probably because I was hungry. I wished I was already at Bensu's, that I would be freed from that minibus, freed from those throngs of poor unfortunate people who had fled from so-called "state terror" and brought their filth to this city, freed from that bastard's staring, and not least freed from the arabesque music on the radio. Pîra NAH kept giggling like a schoolgirl.

* * *

As with many other things, Yasemîn and I frequently disagreed when it came to the topic of the *Easterners*. For one thing, each of us came to our arguments from entirely different perspectives. Whenever the topic of those abject people came up, we'd go to war with each other like lawyers pleading our cases. I'll never forget, one night, she practically grabbed me by the collar and just went off, all because of one single ill-timed word—I never called them Kurds, never called it Kurdistan—and she went ballistic; her words felt like a slap in the face: "Every time you call Kurdistan *The Southeast* in that indifferent tone of yours, all I can think of is the weather reporter coming on the screen after a bunch of propaganda-filled news reports." She'd bicker with our father in the exact same way, especially when the martyrs were shown on the news. Both of us were in Enqere then, living with our parents. That was a whole separate issue, of course; I was the youngest, born of their fear of an empty nest. A long story, complicated too. I'd ask them, "Why don't we have any brothers? Did Dad really not want any?"

As for family's roots, my parents' origins, one's an émigré and the other's a Kurd. So why would my dad always insist, "Biz Türküz kızım"? Every time he said that, "Biz Türküz kızım,"—"We're Turks, my daughter"—my sister would go mental. Screaming and shouting whatever came out of her mouth, she'd turn and look at my mom, her eyes almost brimming with tears. "Why aren't you saying anything? Why aren't you telling us that we're the children of a Kurdish mother? Isn't it the mother whose lineage matters most?" But my poor mom wouldn't make a sound, wouldn't say yes or no to either my dad or my sister; she'd just lower her head and sink into her thoughts.

* * *

That night I told Bensu the story of my relationship with Onder, from the very beginning to its anticlimactic end. We were in her room; she was in bed, I on the couch across from her. It had started to rain again, but the cold didn't really get inside. In addition to the two of us, her parents and her brother, five years younger than her, were home. Her dad had turned off the lights to watch TV in the living room while the others went to sleep. Past midnight, I still hadn't finished telling her the whole sordid tale. Bensu suggested we go to sleep; I didn't know why at first, but then we heard her dad's voice from the other room. "Bensu, daughter, don't you have a test in the morning? Go to bed already!"* That barb was aimed at me. Though Bensu entreated me to keep pouring out my heart, I didn't feel like talking anymore.

"Good night," I said to her, and laid my head on my pillow.

* Bensu's dad yells at her in Turkish—"Bensu, kızım senin sabah sınavın yok muydu? Uyusan artık!"—because of course he does, because he's a cop, and all cops are bastards. (Trans.)

"Be glad your dad's not a cop," Bensu said as she put out the light before conking out.

No, my dad wasn't a cop or a soldier; he'd managed a bank for many years. He had retired before Yasemîn started her job at the university and now spent all his time at home, loafing around my mother, whose life he had wasted and would continue to waste. The silver lining was that his hegemony over us, and especially the iron fist with which he ruled over our sweet mother, had dwindled due to Yasemîn's interference. She had forced him to take a step back, and thanks to her, his heavy man's voice which once drowned out our mother's now fell silent. That's the kind of person my sister was. "I'm going to leave everything behind and join up with the guerrillas," she threatened, after which he became a completely different person. Yasemîn had been bluffing, of course, but she had triumphed because of it.

* * *

The following morning, Bensu and I left her house without eating anything and walked to the bus stop. She apologized again for her father. I smiled as I kissed her on her rosy cheeks and said goodbye.

It was still early, and I wanted to call Yasemîn. Before long, the minibus arrived, and I was met by the same poor people, the same weary faces, the same music, the same stale air. Their eyes glued to my body, of course. Not to mention the nausea. I'd had similar feelings on a train I took from the city of Mêrsîn to the city of Edene. When the train passed by the Easterners' neighborhood, those dirty kids threw stones at it from the side of the tracks. One of the passengers, unable to restrain himself, leaned out his window to chastise them: "Enemies of prosperity! Enemies of the state!" A few others in the compartment cheered him on.

Why were they doing it?

What was their problem?

Do people become enemies of prosperity for no reason?

Do they want to smash the windows of the train because they're poor?

When I asked Yasemîn, her reply puzzled me. "It's not because they're poor or because they're *enemies of prosperity*; it's because the train represents power. Their problem is with people who have power; they're showing that even though they're just kids, they won't surrender to those more powerful than them. The train's nothing more than a symbol, especially since it was carrying Kurds too."

* * *

He sat across from Yasemîn, sipping on his cooling cup of coffee, going on and on in his low-pitched voice, telling her about something in an excited and almost nervous state.

"Morning!"

"Morning!"

"This is my little sister, Merasîm," Yasemîn said.

"And I'm *Sertac Karan*," he replied, extending his hand.

How could I have known that hand was a hand that belonged to someone who wasn't all there?[1]

And that it wasn't extended to me with the best of intentions?[2]

PART ONE
Faith

1

"AND ACCORDING TO a different story, the source of the written word is *Miracle*, which is to say the *Divine*. For it was *His Holiness Adam* who created all alphabets. *His Holiness Adam* recorded these alphabets on tablets, and after *Prophet Noah*'s flood, every nation found its written word and began to read," says Teacher Sertac, quickly glancing at the notebook in front of him to check whether or not anything he said had been incorrect. Upon seeing he had correctly quoted what was written, he uses a piece of chalk to write these claims in his elegant handwriting on the blackboard already covered in words and shapes: "*For it was His Holiness Adam who created all alphabets.*"

Alî Osman's obnoxious voice pipes up. "Wow, can you believe Teacher forgot to say *Peace be upon Him* yet again? How many times before he remembers?" The other students begin to laugh; Sertac pretends not to hear that shithead, doesn't even turn around. Instead, he blows the chalk dust off his fingertips and looks at his Citizen watch. "Still time," he says to himself. "Still another fifteen minutes."

Is it the fact that he is *right-here-right-now* that makes the situation unbearable, or is it the fact that he isn't *elsewhere-and-elsewhen*? He can't decide. He doesn't want to let on that his patience is spent. "You're free to go," he tells the class in a half-dead voice, and goes to sit in his chair, which is covered in chalk dust.

He sits there and watches his students. He looks furtively at the side of the room where the girls sit. Seventeen girls, all gathered on the left side. They're polite and well-behaved, quiet, calm, very shy. They have pious names like *Rabîa* and *Hebîbe* and *Aleyna* and *Zeyneb* and *Xeyrûnîsa* and *Fatîma* and *Umeyye* and *Mûslîme*, and some are pretty and some are ugly, and not a one of them even looks at him, much less makes eye contact with him.

It's weird: When they lift their fingers to answer a question and stand up, they look at the board, even if there's nothing written on it, and speak so softly, they're damn near impossible to hear. At first, he had thought this a gesture of disrespect toward a teacher who wasn't part of the *Community of Believers* and hadn't paid it much more heed than that. But after studying up on the subject, especially the relevant *hadith*, he realized it had nothing to do with disrespect or timidness. Nothing whatsoever, in fact; the issue was in the *gaze*, in the meaning of the gaze. According to most Islamic jurists, it was considered makruh for a woman to look at a man who's a stranger, apart from certain exceptional circumstances, and the girls considered him to be a stranger.

And they're odd; they've practically grown hunchbacks from all their reading and memorizing, and they're starting to go blind. They're constantly reading. Even now they're reading the Qur'an; he can tell from their muttering. Memorizing its *surahs* and *ayahs*, its *hadith*, its *poetry*, its *turns of phrase*. They're practically killing themselves over the agitative stories, poetry, and sermons, which seemed to him a mirage beyond his sight. Many, though not all, came from well-off families; he could tell by their clothes and designer headscarves. Still, they were nothing like the stuck-up, temperamental girls at the other school where he'd interned as a teacher.

And on the right, the boys sit beneath the tall window with its iron grate. All of them, including Alî Osman, keep themselves busy. Some of them, like the ones named *Îmadeddîn* and *Carullah* and *Zekeriyya* and *Mûcahîd* and *Kaddafî*, are reading the Qur'an like the girls on the left; the others use small pocketknives hidden in their palms to *scritch* and *scratch* and *scritch* and *scratch* the names of *God* and the shapes of hearts and flowers and guns and handcuffs onto their desks, which belong, after all, to the state. They don't realize that their teacher can see them doing this—just like God above, of course—but as usual isn't saying anything, doesn't even want to say anything.

He will stop himself from saying these thoughts aloud. He imagines what they would all look like if he were to speak them into being. The scene goes something like this: Bewildered, silent, they will stop what they're doing and turn to look at him, stare at him like deer in headlights. They will suddenly fail to recognize who he is, or what he means to say with these proclamations. Here's what he will say: "No need to carve *His Names* into the property of the state, *The Lord of All the World* makes His presence felt to us in every form and in every place;

in fact, He appeared last year up at the peak of Mount Ercîyes. Just this year He appeared in someone's palm in Şirnex. Haven't you heard that He makes His appearances in the shell of a pistachio, inside a tomato, or likewise in the scales of a fish or in the comb of a beehive or in the yolk of an egg?"

Why can't he bring himself to say such things? Is he afraid of someone? Whom? Unanswered questions, questions that seize hold of his collar before the bell rings and take him back, years earlier, to an *unfinished story*. No, he won't resist, he'll let himself be carried away, even if his heart's not in it.

2

DESPITE THE FACT that his instructor, *may God bless her*, had let Sertac peek at the answer key to fully one hundred percent of the correct answers to the math questions, Sertac didn't pass the university entrance exam that year. "The questions weren't so easy, and my state of mind hasn't really been great," he'd said to his friends who had passed the test. A few days before the test, he'd gone to Sheikh* Spyglass—not empty-handed, of course—to learn whether he would pass. When he met Sheikh Spyglass at the door of his sacred chamber, the Sheikh yelled at him, shooing him away and telling him not to come back again.

* Much to my chagrin, the word "Sheikh," like many other words from the so-called *Middle East*, and especially those having to do with Islam, arrives into English from Arabic rather than from Kurdish. Sheikh is likely more familiar to you, dear reader, than the Kurdish "Şêx"; this word, and others like it that have slipped into common English usage, occupies this text the way that Kurdistan is occupied by Arab countries: unwillingly, and with a tyranny only surpassed by the Republic of Turkey. (Trans.)

Sheikh Spyglass probably saw something in Sertac's eyes. A bad omen, ill fortune, his lack of preparedness? But that day, Sheikh Spyglass must have worn his spectacles backward, because after sending away Sertac, he declared to nobody in particular, "You're going to fail, don't even try!"

That year, he was left all alone in Zerdav. His friends who'd passed the exam eventually gave up their hope in him, and so they slowly cut him off as they left for other places. He started working at a bookshop run by a mullah friend of his, in order to save himself from the tyranny of his parents. He didn't do it for money or anything. He just wanted to spend entire days there, wandering from one dusty shelf to another in that narrow, somber shop. He'd take the books off the shelves one by one, wipe the dust first off the shelves, then off the covers. There were a couple hundred religious books there, never more and never less. Apart from the mullah's son, Xelîlko—God had given the boy shit for brains—and the occasional drowsy-eyed hadji, almost nobody came in. Xelîlko would come by to mooch money from Sertac, which was why every day of the Lord he found himself having to tussle with Xelîlko. He couldn't bring himself to complain to his friend the mullah about the boy, until one day, he let slip by accident that the boy was annoying him; but, after all, he said, Xelîlko was merely human, and humans make mistakes, even in the Holy Qur'an. The sentence had barely left his mouth when the mullah brought a wallop of such force against Xelîlko's face that he was flung against the shelves, and the shelves along with the books on them toppled down *kablam* on the boy. Sertac's heart leapt to his throat; he didn't know what to do, whether he should restrain his friend or run to Xelîlko's aid; he did the latter, not heeding his friend the mullah who told him to stop, and pulled the wretched Xelîlko from under the shelves. Sertac felt so guilty, and from that day forth decided to do better by Xelîlko.

After two days' absence, Xelîlko slinked back into the shop, but this time, Sertac showered him in kindness. His friend the mullah had gone to the muftiate to take care of some business that would last all day, so the shop had been left, as usual, to him and Xelîlko. After a warm greeting, he seated Xelîlko on the boss's stool behind the counter and ran to the shop to get him an ice-cold *Yedigün*,* leaving Xelîlko salivating with pleasure. With this bribe he seized upon an opportunity he'd been scheming up for days. When Xelîlko tried to bum some more money off of him, Sertac would reply first by giving him religious advice; he'd scare the boy with talk of *djinns*, of *devils*, of *Gogs* and *Magogs*, and then ask him a series of questions. These questions would go as follows: What was his father doing to his poor mother, who, rumor had it, was an Êzidî forcibly converted to Islam? Had Xelîlko seen anything? The plan began to work, and Xelîlko, unsatisfied with his single *Yedigün*, asked for more money. Sertac counted out some loose change he'd stolen from his mother over the past couple of days, and Xelîlko began chirping like a nightingale: "She's not my real mom, *Uncle Sertac*... She and my dad go in the bathroom together, *Uncle Sertac*..." and he stuck

* Yedigün is a Turkish brand of soda; the name translates to "Sevenday," and it comes in orange, tangerine, and lemon flavors. Imagine Fanta that tastes somehow both more sugary and much worse, and with a less catchy jingle to boot. (Trans.)

his hand in his pocket and pulled out a little jar. "What's this, *Uncle Sertac*? I ate some of it, but it didn't taste like anything." What he held in his hands was a jar of *Vaseline*.*

Sertac felt worse for Xelîlko as the boy went on. He felt worse for all the poor, pitiful kids like Xelîlko; Zerdav was full of them. Xelîlko was a few bricks shy of a load; "because of the beatings," Sertac told himself. But these were no ordinary beatings; the beatings were so heinous, so blasphemous, that if you saw the boy before the scrapes and bruises from his previous beatings had fully healed, you'd think he must have been attacked by dogs. One day he asked his friend the mullah about the beatings. Would that he had swallowed his tongue instead! It had never once crossed his mind that his friend could completely rip him a new asshole using words he'd never even heard before. Sertac, the mullah said, was an *adem-î qebûl*. Didn't accept things as they were. Closed his eyes to the truth. Refused the truth, in fact, without ever even considering what the truth might actually be. Things quickly escalated from the mullah's beatings of Xelîlko, snowballing out of his control. Sertac wasn't obligated to listen, of course; he could leave, but he didn't, instead subjecting himself to his friend's strange words as he prattled on and on: "People like you have what I call *cehl-î murekeb*, complex ignorance. There are two types of ignorance: The first is *cehl-î basît*, simple ignorance, the ignorance we know; the other, *cehl-î*

* Vaseline is an oil-based lubricant that first appeared on the market in 1870 as "Vaseline Petroleum Jelly." Health experts recommend against the use of Vaseline as a lubricant during sexual intercourse, much less for eating, but who are you to judge? (Trans.)

murekeb, is for someone so ignorant, they don't even realize they're ignorant. It's easy to treat *cehl-î basît*, not a problem at all; as for *cehl-î murekeb*, it's practically impossible. Ignorance is a sickness, and you are ignorant, Sertac, you are sick! You think you're smarter than everyone else, but you don't even realize that your *nefs*, your *ego*, is also a sickness. The Devil himself is an emissary of the *nefs*, and it's clear to me he's pissed all over your soul. You ask me why I beat Xelîlko? It's none of your business, that's why! What do you care anyway?"

No, indeed, it was none of Sertac's business; still, he thought about replying:

"All right, so what's your *complex* then?"

And he thought about saying:

"There's no *ego* more disgusting than your *ego*!"

And he thought about and wanted to say so much more, but instead he bit his tongue and left the shop. Silent, he made for the hell back home, from which there was no return.

Pîra NAH's cackles resounded in his head.

As he made his way home, for reasons he couldn't quite figure out, tears began streaming down his face.

3

HE TURNS HIS attention to the course book; they've barely started the third month of classes and it's already falling apart from negligence. The cover, scrawled over with random doodles, is beginning to fall off. He glances over the pages, the other teachers' signatures, the different kinds of handwriting, the titles of courses and their accompanying assignments. He coughs a few times, trying to clear the itch in his throat, and tears well up. He wonders what the philosophy teacher, Hûrî Xanim, would say; he ran into her at lunch yesterday on his way into the teachers' lounge, and they talked awhile about his throat problem. "You've got laryngitis, Sertac," Hûrî Xanim said to him, and then with the demeanor of a pedigreed doctor she listed off the many and varied symptoms of the condition and advised him to cut back on smoking—though it'd be best to quit altogether, of course. No, he can't do it. He can't quit cold turkey. He is the kind of man who burns through his cigarettes, even during Ramadan. Certainly not in the teachers' lounge, though, not for the whole *Community of Believers* to see! Every ten minutes or so he would go to the computerless computer room and shamelessly roll a cigarette. Up till now, nobody—not a soul!—had said anything to him about the fact that he didn't fast or pray. Nor had they ever asked him whether he believed in God. From day one they had taken a liking to him, hadn't bothered him, hadn't interrupted him, hadn't asked about his past. One day he might mention Ibn Khaldun's *Mukeddîme*, the next, he might talk about Seyîd Qutb's *Fîzilal'îl Qur'an*; he might draw everyone's attention by his use of the concept of *parrhesia*, his commitment to truth; or else he might tell them "I am a socialist Muslim" with as much sincerity as he could muster. He had gone to their homes, sat at their tables, met their spouses. And yet, despite that, he felt ill at ease. Either he was exceedingly apprehensive, or else there was something to them he couldn't quite put his finger on that gave him reason to be distrustful.

It had been a hot September day two years earlier when, diploma in hand, wearing his first—and at the time only—two-piece suit, oversized and faded as it was, along with his newly polished shoes, too small for his feet, he climbed the marble stairs of the school, beads of sweat on his broad, shining forehead, and entered underneath the weather-worn sign with the school's name. He hadn't yet been made the art teacher. Because before any of the new hires could become proper *teachers*, they would have to impress the principal and department heads, and eventually the *Community of Believers* as well, especially the most zealous among them; as a consequence the new hires were hopeless, effectively interns. No, the Imam

Hatip School for training imams and clerics wasn't his cup of tea,* nor had he come there of his own volition. But his father, Fethî (*Fethî the Postman*), gave him the most fatherly advice in order to get him to start working and look to the future, and beyond that to ease his own mind. "In the end, it's a school, it's tied to the ministry, so what does it matter to you what they do there? You go, you teach, and you leave. So go already, go and get to work!"

Sertac dug in his feet, though, deciding to throw a tantrum. "You're throwing your son to a bunch of stark-raving fundamentalists! Me and religion, me and Imam Hatip? What am I supposed to do there, pray and fast? I don't even know how to perform ablutions. I haven't the slightest idea what direction Mecca is, and now you're telling me to go to the Imam Hatip School. Why would I go? If you think it's so easy, why don't you go instead? Go on already, here's my diploma!"

His father glared back at him. "Good Lord, you're a fool. God as my witness, it's as though I'm telling you there's not a cloud in the sky and you're convinced it's going to rain. My boy, my son, please listen to your dad; you won't be on your own, there's bound to be many others like you at the school. Fundamentalists, good grief.[3] Get out of here, get out of my sight!"

* One time—I must have been in my early twenties—I was an election observer for one of the now-shuttered Kurdish political parties in a highly contested electoral district in Turkey. The polling station was an Imam Hatip School, and a police officer, upon seeing my credentials, drew his gun and commanded me to exit. This doesn't tell you about what Imam Hatip Schools do, I know, but maybe it tells you something about why they might not be Sertac's "cup of tea." (Trans.)

He continued grumbling. “Fundamentalists, huh? Of course. God, you have no idea how ridiculous you are . . . I don’t give a fuck whether you go or not! God grant me strength, forgive me.” And as his dad said goodbye, he repeated what he said. “You have no choice, son.”

His dad was right; Sertac didn’t have a choice, and for a few months, he would be teaching courses on Husn-î Xet, *Arabic calligraphy*, owing to his skill in all the fine arts except for painting and to his elegant penmanship. But something strange happened on his first day, something he only mentioned to Hûrî Xanim. Nobody told him how he should act in a school of prayer and supplication, nor how he should address students, especially in their first meeting, and so with what he could remember from his on-the-job training, he walked into the classroom—the very one he found himself in now, tearily staring at the tattered course book—as sure of himself as he could be, even a little arrogant, and when the students all stood up with the appearance of the new teacher and waited for his instruction, he proclaimed, a little too loudly and forcefully in Turkish, “Good morning, friends!” But only a few students, one of them being Alî Osman, greeted him back, and so, a little shaken, he walked over to his chair, leaving his pride on the lectern, and busied himself—the same as he was doing now—with whatever was on his desk.

Yes, that’s exactly what had happened. And his father, who had never shown any interest in him either as a child or as an adult, who had never come home with toys, candy, or chocolate for his son, finally acted like a real father and took an interest in solving his problem.[4]

He thought back on his childhood years; what weird fucking times those were.

Thinking about that period of his life, a bitter smile spreads now across his face. His dreams were a thousand times greater than those of his mom, his dad, his brother, his uncle, his dimwit aunt, and the collectively bankrupt, down-and-out people of Zerdav, but he can't figure out why.

4

SERTAC WAS A poor child who came into the world in the Lower Quarter of Zerdav one hot summer day. He had neither family nor tribe to be proud of, except for Neil Armstrong, who set foot on the Moon the day he was born. The hero Neil was a dear friend to Sertac,* riding on his Apollo 11 every night to come visit and tell Sertac stories of the Moon, of his journey there and the reasons he stayed there, and, especially, of its craters, until Sertac fell asleep.

Sertac's father, Fethî (*Fethî the Postman*), worked in the Zerdav post office, and according to his calculations, in precisely four years, six months, and fourteen days, *should God and the Prophet permit*, he would buy a big, breezy, sun-filled house in the Upper Quarter, one with working sinks, for the kids.

At the time, Sertac was barely six years old and hadn't yet started school. On sunny, beautiful days he would go with his

* Unfortunately, because of Neil Armstrong's untimely demise, this claim could not be independently verified. (Trans.)

dim-witted older brother, Nizam, to the square in the Lower Quarter. There he'd scuffle with the other kids, wanting to play ball. After making pretend peace with them, he'd run after the rubber ball that was the treasure of the Upper Quarter kids until the sun set. He and his brother would return home filthy, walk from the gravel road to the water drum, careful and afraid, and rinse their faces, before going inside to sit down to dinner with the rest of the family.

His brother ate whatever was put in front of him without objection, even if it was no more than cheese and bread to sate him. But even as a young boy, Sertac had a refined palate, wanting to eat meat at every meal, and his mother would give him a tongue-lashing every time. "You and Fethî, men who eat meat! You think you're worth more than sweet Nizam? Shut up and eat! You don't like it? You can eat Nizam's balls!"

At that, Sertac would usually leave the table and put a spoonful of **EVET*** oil on his bread, topping it off with powdered sugar and eating it slowly without making a sound. If he made a sound, he knew his mom would appear, slipper in hand, *what do you think you're eating*, and beat him till kingdom come. When that happened, Nizam pretended like he had to study, taking himself into the big room where the *Ataturk*** poster hung on the wall and staring at that poster for hours without coming out.

* Evet: the Turkish word for "yes," and also the name of a brand of cooking oil once widespread in Kurdistan. (Trans.)

** Astute readers will note the absence of the umlaut in Ataturk's name here. No such letter exists in the Kurdish language. Given Sertac's own insistence on the mortal difference a diacritic makes; given Turkey's decades-long prohibition on the letters X, W, and Q, which *are* in the

Nizam wasn't anywhere near as brave as Sertac. The moment he got a whiff of a coming beating, he would piss himself and succumb to tears, his cries earsplitting, *wah wah wah*. Though she knew Nizam would have pissed himself, their mother never could bring herself to use her slipper on him to punish him. No, it was always the same story: Sertac had poured water from the pitcher on Nizam's pants; it was his fault, not Nizam's.

Their mom doted on Nizam; he was her one and only. She would stroke his head, always buzzed bald and covered in bruises, comforting him with sweet words; she would always call him to her so she could read him a juz from the Qur'an. Was Nizam her only child? What about Sertac? One day the aunt his mother hated said to Sertac, "He stole your mother's milk, little lamb." But how could a mother's milk be stolen? Sertac poured his heart out to Neil, hoping the astronaut would bring him to the Moon and find him a mother who wouldn't beat him with her slipper. A mother who would love him, who would feed him meat and bananas.[5]

One day he asked Neil if there were bananas on the Moon. Neil smiled and replied to his friend, "Well, of course there are. That's where the best, most delicious bananas are." Sertac continued with his line of questioning. "Do you know why I asked?" Neil clicked his tongue and shook his head. "How would I know, Sertac?" Sertac whispered into Neil's ear, "Because . . .

Kurdish alphabet but not in the Turkish alphabet; given that Kurds have been arrested and criminally prosecuted for using these letters; and given that Ataturk is the father of Turkey's language policy, we should feel comfortable withholding from him the courtesy of his umlaut. (Trans.)

I've never eaten a banana." The sentence broke Neil's heart. He put his hand on the Holy Qur'an and swore that on his next visit he would bring Sertac Moon bananas.

Neil kept his word, and though he couldn't come himself, three days later, his promised bananas arrived. Sertac's father appeared at the door carrying a bag full of bananas, and Sertac threw himself on the ground in front of him and began screaming, "Dad, bananas! Dad, bananaaaas! Dad, baaaaanaaanaaaaas!" But before his father could even reply, his mother cut in. "What's all this going *bananas for bananas*, you miserable little wretch?" His share of the bag that night would be barely half a banana, but he lost no time in consuming it—he was so excited about it, in fact, he hadn't been able to eat his dinner. He went into the big room where the poster of Ataturk was hanging and smelled the banana for a long time, then licked it like it was ice cream, which didn't give him much pleasure. Then, afraid of Nizam, he put the whole thing in his mouth and swallowed before going to ask his mom for the banana peel. In addition to the half a banana that night, he ate not one, not two, but three blows from his mom's cruel slipper, and though he went to bed to "conk out," sleep, as usual, wouldn't come.

The whole family slept in the same room. His bed was next to Nizam's, a few meters from the stove, while his parents' was farther away and right by the stove. His mom started whispering, and in no time those whispers turned into sighs and moans, reaching Sertac's pricked-up ears in waves; in the darkness Sertac couldn't figure out what was happening, who was doing what to whom. Whatever they did, some weeks after he heard those whispers, his mother's stomach began swelling up. As it did, the kids of the Lower Quarter began talking about her.

The kids of the Lower Quarter had such filthy mouths; it was truly shameful. Never mind the way they competed to out-swear one another's moms and sisters, all for a top or a tigereye marble! They could rattle off their swears so fast, Sertac could seldom figure out who said what and what was said to whom. Those who had sisters had an advantage over those who didn't—for the time being, he was one of the latter. Because it would always start with other kids' sisters, then their moms, followed by aunts and sisters-in-law and even cousins; sometimes it even reached all the way to grandmas. It was quite possible to gain a comprehensive education in the full anatomy of a woman by way of these expletives. Sure, they were joking, but when the jokes turned to shit and people started throwing punches and rocks, someone was almost always left in tears. Somebody would get a black eye or start bleeding, and it always made Sertac's stomach churn. He had to practically run in circles to avoid the rocks they rained down on one another.

Cusses and *rocks* were both things Neil did not tolerate, and he had promised Sertac he would purge the Lower Quarter of all cusses and rocks. But he was not well. In fact, he was fighting off disease. One night, he turned to Sertac, his only friend in the world, and choked out his tragic prognosis. "It's cancer." He asked Sertac for a prayer rug and the Qur'an and whispered, "Ablutions." Sertac ran to fetch the prayer rug and the Qur'an, and after thanking him, Neil took the book with a dramatic flourish and placed it next to the prayer rug. After he prayed, he read a few ayahs from the Qur'an, his voice soft and weepy. Because the time had come to say goodbye, and Neil was truly *overcome* with emotion. He gestured for Sertac to come close.

Closer. There was something he needed to tell Sertac. It was a strange and devastating scene, Neil in a fetal position on the prayer rug. They both waited for death to arrive, when suddenly, and in an instant, it did, and his color faded away.

5

HE CHECKS HIS Citizen watch a second, a third, a fourth time, but the time is not passing, the minute hand is stuck in place and not moving a single tick. Why is he so impatient, so restless? Does he have somewhere to go? Where? Who is expecting him? He glances at the course book and closes it, begins drawing shapes in his own notebook out of dread and anger. Having to look at Alî Osman and his crew is beginning to really rile him up. Alî Osman, right now in the middle of scratching his nutsack, is pinning to the board a picture of Palestinian children killed in an airstrike on their school and wondering what reaction Teacher will have. He and Alî Osman had squabbled over the photograph, and Sertac had already taken the photograph off the board and delivered it back to its owner. How old was Alî Osman when the Helebçe Massacre happened? Was it possible he'd never heard of it?

A few months earlier, Sertac had found himself in the Old City. He went to learn the fate of a petition he'd given to the directorate already four weeks ago now. For an hour, an hour and a half, he had paced up and down the pale white corridors of that faceless building without finding an administrator or getting a single signature. He passed from one room to the next, coming face-to-face in each room with middle-aged women sitting behind desks, all countenanced in bizarre makeup. However many techniques there are for chewing gum in the world, he encountered each and every last one there. Hyenas waiting to retire, all of them, so busy fretting over their lunchtime shish kebabs, they didn't even turn to look at him. Soon as he realized he couldn't get the job done, he left that insane asylum, swearing all the way, and made for the humble marketplace in the Old City. It had been a long time since he'd eaten one of those home-cooked meals there, stew with lots of broth and lots of meat. Looking for a restaurant, he came upon a stand in a crowded square where six girls in headscarves were gathering donations for the Palestinians, accompanied by Arabic music that resounded in the air. One of them caught his attention, a beautiful, short, blue-eyed girl, her face bright as the Moon, and so he walked right up to the girl and, in clear Turkish, spoke quickly and nervously to her.

"Good luck, sister. Looks to me like you're raking in donations. Good, I'm glad. Truly, the people of Palestine have suffered incomparable cruelty, a cruelty that is still ongoing. But when I saw you, I thought of something, something not quite as far away. Rumor has it that *Count Saddam* murdered a hundred and eighty thousand Muslim Kurds during his *Enfal* campaign. I bet you've heard of him, and there's surely no need for me to talk at length about *Helebçe*. My question is this: How many Arab states, including Palestine, raised their voices in objection to this massacre, which blew Hiroshima out of the water? Let me tell you: not a single one. Why? Yes, why? Is God not One? Was God not One then? I will never entrust my faith to a God who is Arab!"

He turned his back and fled quickly, without seeing how *sister* reacted, darting down one of the narrow streets to cover his tracks.

Yes, his words had come straight from his heart; he didn't regret a single one. Half an hour after this incident, he sat in a restaurant along the main road, dipping his bread in meaty broth as he watched the pimple-faced waiter clicking the remote at the television, looking for music videos. When he landed on a news channel the boss intervened, asking him to change the channel, and Sertac felt the same thing again. The screen was plastered with more crushing news about Israel's war on the Palestinians. Five Palestinian children had been shot point-blank in a school, and their families were beating themselves with grief. He called out to the waiter, the knot in his throat making his voice weepy. "Good Lord, is this humanity? It's blasphemy, it's barbarity! What do they want from those babies?"

Sertac had lost his taste for the stew, just as he would lose sleep that night. One nightmare followed the other. In his nightmare that night, he saw that beautiful, short, blue-eyed girl from the square in the Old City, her face bright as the Moon, in one of God's many palaces, waiting on guests from around the world who had come to enjoy themselves. Everyone there from near and far spoke, their voices coalescing into a loud roar, and no matter how much blood they guzzled at the hands of that nymphet, their thirst was never sated. It was the blood of the have-nots and there was no end to it. Members of The People's Brotherhood Choir, conducted by what looked like Gustav Mahler, sang "The Internationale." Count Saddam and Yasser played a game of chess in the middle of the hall. And what a game it was! Instead of pawns, severed heads: the heads of children, women, the elderly, the brave, the mad, and even the heads of chickens, dogs, and cows. He could see with his own two eyes what they were doing to those withered craniums, those bodiless shrunken heads.

* * *

Except for a few teachers who were Kurdish—himself one, the history teacher, Mihemed, from Lîcê two, the Turkish Language and Literature teacher, Uncle Şehabedîn, from Muş three, the English teacher, Alîye Xanim, who was an Elewî from Dersim four—most of the faculty was composed of Turkish members of the *Community of Believers*, from Central Anatolia, who had been working at the school for a long time. The principal, a couple of vice principals, some officers in the school's parent-teacher association, some workers in the cafeteria, a few active imams, a handful who opened stores and had built too many relationships, and, of course, a few who would eventually go on to become car salesmen. Cheerily, pleased with themselves, they made idle conversation with one another. They were thick as thieves with the people of the region, close as two coats of paint. The stories and anecdotes shared in the teachers' lounge, and the jokes told, always had the same punch line, and that punch line was always pious and moralizing. But as soon as the Kurdish question[*] came up, the conviviality they had shared just moments ago would collapse into a strange discomfort. "They're not going to spend their whole lives here," Sertac consoled himself. "They'll leave, return to Aqseray or Yozgat or Qonya or Qirşehir or Çorum or Çanqiri or Nîgde or Qeyserî—they all leave sooner or later."

His cough is getting worse.[6] He opens his leather bag and roots around for a pack of tissues. Pens and pencils of all kinds emerge from the pockets in the bag. A pack of cigarettes, along with three lighters. An eraser; an old, short ruler; three cartridges of ink for the fountain pen that got clogged some time ago and is now functionally useless; a palmful of loose change; a paper clip; passport pictures that will surely come in handy any day now; a box of colored chalk. "A little bit of everything," he mutters to himself with not a little anger, "except for the cheapest and most essential thing." Now he'll either have to cover his mouth with his hand, or he'll have no choice but to ask for a tissue from the students. What an embarrassment. Unable to restrain himself, he turns to the girls again; losing himself in thought, he descends into the darkest depths of his childhood.

* A truly dazzling euphemism for what happens when the Kurds resist their wholesale erasure, no matter violent or nonviolent. As a still more famous question asks: *What is to be done?* The "Kurdish question" is a question to which the only acceptable answer, at least to the state of Turkey, is to stop with all this Kurdistan shit. (Trans.)

6

HE LIED TO *Little Îhsan*, *Little Murad*, *Little Whosit*, and *Little Whatsit*, the troublemaking children of the Lower Quarter, each peskier and more worthless than the last. He told them he was bringing a photographer to take portraits of each of them, *click click*—never mind the who, the where, or the why—all so he could sneak away that day and join the group of girls assembled in the square, playing quietly, calmly, noiselessly, and peacefully under the shade of the fig tree across from his house. He announced, "I'm *Doctor Sertac*, here to take care of you all," then proclaimed himself the *pretend* husband of birdbrained dummy *Little Taybet* with the words "I'm your *pretend* husband, and you're my *pretend* wife," and, assuring her with the words "You're my *pretend* patient too," he took his new *pretend* spouse by his side, and together they went to visit all the *pretend* sick *pretend* neighbors whose *pretend* husbands had gone to *pretend* war for the real Yavru Vatan,* that is, for Cyprus—the map of Cyprus is *so* weird!—and hadn't returned. Many of our men have been martyred, they said to one another, and so many from around here too, they continued, drinking their *pretend* tea and *pretend* Kool-Aid. He held ten *pretend* cups, and blew on them all for his *pretend* neighbors, all girls, upon which he told them to lie facedown on the ground, and after they did what he asked, more than a little begrudgingly, Sertac lifted the girls' skirts to see where he would give them their *pretend* shots, and as he looked at their bare pink bottoms with intentions that had no good in them at all, he said, "Your case is dire, dear neighbor, *tsk tsk tsk tsk*, I need to kiss your *bumbum* or else you're gonna die," at which time he muttered something sounding *Turkish* and officious, *bilmebilmem*. They didn't make a peep, poor things, no, until *mwah* and *mwah* and a third *mwah* and then screams rang out. *Little Taybet*, his pretend spouse, grabbed a rock from the ground, and no sooner had she slammed it down on Sertac's head than his traitorous wife, *ugh God*, yelled at

* Yavru Vatan (Turkish): a name meaning "Baby Homeland," referring to Cyprus, which Turkey invaded in 1974. For more than fifty years, the island has been partitioned, and the only state that recognizes the Turkish Republic of Northern Cyprus is the Republic of Turkey. In 2015, describing the ossified state of dependency that Northern Cyprus has on Turkey, and calling for the reunification of Cyprus, the president of Northern Cyprus asked the press, "Will we always be baby [yavru]?" It's worth noting that "yavru" seldom refers to a human baby; rather, it is the generic term for a baby animal—think kitten, puppy, cub, duckling. I imagine Northern Cyprus as the runt of the litter among Turkey's sprawling imperial ambitions: neglected by its mother, cast out of its nest, starving to death. Nice beaches, though. (Trans.)

the other dummy on the ground, "Girl, are you stupid? He got you pregnant!" at which point she erupted in a *hair-raising, heartrending* cry, sobbing pitifully as she ran all the way home, while *Doctor Sertac*, with a childish obstinacy and rancor and above all with a sharp pain in his head, stormed through the *pretend* houses and rooms and courtyards and kitchens the girls had built out of so many crooked lines and dots and circles in the sand, out of big shiny stones and rocks, kicking and punching to destroy everything they had assembled—a few old, dirty, busted, broken toys gathered from the dumpster by the military base, along with the rags, wood, and tin they used to divide the sections of their *beautifully pretend* homes—shouting slogans the whole time. Once he'd managed to cheer up, he began soaring home, *freedom, freedom*!

Yes, by God, with that same excitement he climbed the ladder onto the roof and went to his dimly lit hiding spot. It was built out of twelve **EVET** oil cans and constructed in such a manner that he could hide inside and observe through a tiny hole, as if through a spyglass, what was going on outside for hours on end, and Sertac now dedicated himself to monitoring what was going on in the wake of his attack, *yes, all by yourself*.

The group of dummies down there was in the process of putting things back together. His darling *Little Taybet* was engaged in *reconstruction*, while his *pretend* patient *Little Lastîk*—for she had returned to the group—and her two friends, *Little Fincan* and *Little Emo*, came together like *ladybugs* and gathered up all the things that he had kicked and broken while he swore and cursed, placing them all *piece by piece* back into place according to their outlines in the sand. Sertac, on the other hand, proud in his hiding spot, was in the midst of plotting new schemes and scheming new plots, cooking up new lies, new tricks, a feeling he came to pleasantly associate with the sweet taste of fresh-baked *mahmilhewa*. This was his first discovery: Lying made him happy, even if he didn't quite know yet what good his lies did him. *Lying* and *happiness*; he increasingly did not know which came first, which was cause and which was consequence; he just kept making up lies, and would not stop lying, to himself, to his friends, to his pregnant mother and his carefree father, to his older brother, Nizam, to his teachers—he would simply not stop lying.

It was the time of black bags and white collars.

It was the age of *Alî gel* and *Alî koş*.*

Alî was always and ever *gel*-ing and *koş*-ing on the blackboard, always and ever *coming* and *running*.

And Sertac was always in pursuit, with his huge, black eyes.

* These phrases are equivalent to the stock language of the *Dick and Jane* books, once used to teach American children to read: "Run, Dick, run," except Dick lives under martial law. (Trans.)

7

"THE BELL RANG! Hey, Teach, the bell rang!"

Alî Osman's voice tears Sertac from his memories and returns him to the classroom. The boy is the only one standing, a shit-eating grin plastered across his face; the others still sit at their desks, awaiting permission to leave. The bell rings nonstop; the final bell. With slow movements, he closes his notebook and gets himself ready to leave as well. He gives his students permission to exit the classroom. But then, something happens that has never happened before; he does something he has never done before. Before they leave, he says to the students with an air of exaggerated pomp and circumstance, "May God bless you today with all his mercy, bounty, and salutations, boys and girls!"

Teacher Sertac walks hurriedly along a gravel road covered in trash and animal shit. He needs to get home and scarf down something posthaste. Because he hasn't had a bite to eat since morning. Neither the tasteless tea made by Evdila the cafeteria guy nor the crackers past their sell-by date nor the cheese-less sandwiches have passed his lips. The afternoon students pass him in small groups one after another, extravagant in their greetings, showing him deep respect and reverence. They must be in a rush too. He remembers suddenly that he's supposed to go to the doctor. Should he go or not? Should he just make his way down to the market and buy five hundred milligrams of antibiotics straight from the pharmacy, thereby saving himself from the hospital's formalities, and especially from the doctor's smarmy face? He has to make a decision, but he can't. The pain of indecision abates as soon as he reaches the front door of his building, because what sets in now is the sweet, familiar pleasure of *being at home*; he feels like he has arrived right on time, to his *nest*, which makes him feel all the more palpably deep in his gut that he is the happiest person in the world, and that, consequently, he will not go to the doctor, which also means he will not make his way to the market either; he will simply pass through that iron door painted that strange and miraculous shade of green and go upstairs. He will once again eagerly count step after step as he climbs the unstuccoed stairs that he descends and ascends day in and day out, at which point he will find himself at the front door to his home. This home is his home, the home he furnished himself, and aside from a few heavy and rather expensive objects—the laundry machine and dishwasher, the refrigerator, the bedroom furniture, the dining table and chairs, and a few rugs—everything in it belongs to him. Whatever there is inside his house, whether needle or thread, whether bread box or bath soap—to say nothing of all the utterly unspeakable things he owns that a woman ought never to imagine—he had gone and found himself, bought himself, brought home himself. All the things that did women no good,* like books and folders and a paper cutter and pencil cup and ink and inkwell and ruler and compass and set square and protractor, yes, he had bought every last one of them himself.

* * *

And, indeed, it was the house where for a time he and Merasîm fought every last day of the Lord. When it came time to divvy up their belongings, though, he simply lowered his head and fell silent, like his tongue was tied. Having gleaned much wisdom from their past fights, he knew that saying more would hurt her, disappoint her—and she was already so disappointed!—so he didn't want to drag it out.

"I won't live there and let my marriage be poisoned! From the very beginning I kept telling you how dangerous it is there, how detestable, how it's the kind of place where dozens of people are killed, kidnapped, robbed, raped, victimized by terrorists every single day . . . I won't, I won't, I won't!"

Merasîm triplicated herself in exactly this manner.

"I don't want to spend every last day of my life," she continued, "having to look at your mom's face, your dad's face, your brother's face, your sister's face! I won't, I won't, I won't!"[7]

By bringing this up in front of her mother, her father, and Yasemîn, the missus got them mixed up in the ordeal. Her mother

* I suppose I might argue that these things are equally deleterious to the sanity of men, but perhaps it's better to let you discover that for yourself. (Trans.)

realized that things were no good at all, that if her daughter didn't stop being so obstinate, she would soon be a divorcée at the age of twenty-six, which only made her weep and moan even more, and in the end she managed to persuade her sweet little lamb to give it a shot, to go try to live in that "den of terrorists." Yes, Merasîm did come in the end, after Teacher Sertac put that house of his in order; she came one night, dowry chest in tow, to that wild and lawless district and started at her job the very next morning.

* * *

Finding himself in his wifeless and consequently lifeless bedroom, Sertac takes off his faded suit and hangs it up with a kind of ceremonial routine. He goes to the kitchen and sets about doing the same things he always does, as though Merasîm is at home, as though Merasîm never left, never abandoned him and his home, as if Merasîm is still there, as if she's sitting in front of the little TV in the kitchen and he's talking to her, laughing with her, politely asking her for something and she graciously extends it to him, and he observes her, her round face, her cheeks, her pursed lips, her earlobes that wear no earrings, her irises, her hairless, pale-white legs, those nipples of hers he sucked but a short time ago, those knees, those short fingers and their painted fingernails, he looks at the empty space Merasîm left behind, an empty space that since her departure has beaten at his brain and his heart, no, he is entirely out of sorts.

"I'm fucked up," he says aloud for himself to hear. "Idiot, I'm an idiot, such an idiot."

And Pîra NAH replies, "You have no idea, you idiot!"[8]

8

NO, SERTAC REALLY had no idea, *poor Brehîmo*! He had no idea what was going on around him, especially when it came to the daily realities of Zerdav—truly shitty realities—and to what people were being put through, much less the circumstances of this homeland of his which was only called *Kurdistan* in a few poems contained in old *forbidden* books. Neither Fethî (*Fethî the Postman*) nor his mother had ever said to him on a single godforsaken day of his life, "Son, this is our fight against darkness," or "We're Kurds, that's why we're in the midst of all this chaos."* It

* It is reported in the *Şerefname*, the oldest written source on Kurdish history, penned in 1598 by Şerefxan, Emir of Bidlîs, that the Prophet himself is responsible for the misfortunes of the Kurds: "When the call to prophecy of Mihemed, may God's blessings be upon him, and the good news of his mission, caused tumult in all corners of the world, the lords and lofty kings everywhere set out to pay him their obedience and give him their absolute allegiance. Oxuz Xan, in those days one of the grand sultans of Turkistan, sent as an envoy to the fortune-dwelling threshold of the lord of two worlds [the Prophet Mihemed], upon him be the ever-exceeding

was only his youngest uncle, his mother's brother Mihemed, the one who named him *Sertac*, the one who never left them alone at home when his dad wasn't around, the one who ran to their aid whenever he could in Zerdav's brutal winters, the one who always brought two bags full of navel oranges and enormous red apples, it was only that dear uncle of his, wise, understanding, handsome, and softhearted, who would talk about the Kurds, about the situation they found themselves in. And Sertac would grab an apple from his uncle's bags and run to his mother, shouting, "Mom, Mom, Uncle's here, Uncle Mihemed is here!"

His mother would call out to her brother without stopping what she was doing, asking Mihemed to come in. When he'd kneel down to untie the long, tangled laces of his combat boots, Sertac would watch with attentive wonder, dazzled by how quickly those laces passed through those nine eyelets, at which Mihemed would lift his mirthful face and tell him, "I'll get you a pair of boots all your own, I promise. But you have to promise me you'll listen to your mom and dad. Deal?" And he would come in and join his sister, while Sertac would circle and circle those boots, appointing himself their watchman. Sometimes he would wipe off the mud and slip his tiny feet

---

blessings and maximum grace, a Kurdish nobleman named Buxduz—a gigantic, hideous-looking, dark-faced man, to speak for [the sultan's] sincerity of intention and true allegiance. When the hideous-looking envoy appeared in the joy-exuding sight of his holiness, the best of mankind [Prophet Mihemed], He was disgusted and repulsed by his visage. Asking him of his tribe and clan, Buxduz answered: 'I am of the Kurdish nation.' His Holiness said: 'May the pure, exalted Almighty not favor this nation with unity, for otherwise, they shall give the world to ruin.'" (Trans.)

into the boots, becoming thus another one of the revolutionaries sporting black boots and a *Lenin goatee*. Only his uncle would tell him stories about the revolutionaries. Only his uncle would take him down to the Zerdav market and then to the toy store, holding his hand all the while. They were cut from the same cloth, and he loved his uncle more than his father, though when he'd say so to Mihemed he'd get *tsk tsk*s in response. "That's no good! He's your dad. Do you know what they do to kids who don't love their dads? The soldiers come and take them far away, and then . . ."

"And then?" Sertac would reply. "What do they do to the kids?"

His uncle would smile under his mustache. "It's not them but the dogs. They throw the kids as food to the dogs."

Every time Mihemed brought up the soldiers and their dogs, Sertac would be overcome with trembling, and a knot would well up in his throat; but his uncle knew how to tug on Sertac's heartstrings, and he would run his thick fingers through his nephew's hair as he repeated his promise of boots. "Don't cry. They don't do anything to kids. But you do need to show some love to your dad.

"You're just like me, Sertac," he'd continue, "sensitive like me, full of compassion. But the world is not so compassionate; people lack mercy."

Mihemed always wanted to talk about his beloved, a distant cousin of his who married a man from Mêrdîn, to talk about her grace and charm and the misery her betrayal brought him. This was his story, a story he would tell and tell on end. "The Arabs of Mêrdîn are filthy, Sertac. They never wash their dark balls or dirty asses, and they don't wear underwear either. They eat rice with their hands and speak the language of dogs. Savage bastards, all of them, enemies of love!"

So went the story, and Sertac imagined them as he listened: A few Mêrdînîs with tails, bare naked, circled round a dinner table, rolling rice in their hands as they barked at one another and wagged their tails. He had no idea who Arabs were, or what they were, or where they lived. He didn't even know whether or not they were human like he was. But whenever Mihemed's cousin's husband came up, the same images would come to mind and he'd laugh. He felt almost like his uncle was telling him about a cartoon, and he relished listening to the story.

* * *

They never talked about it when Sertac was around, never discussed how or why such a sensitive, compassionate, good-humored man would be killed. They never said who his uncle's murderers were, nor what distinguished him from them. Nobody said a word, they'd just start crying as soon as they saw Sertac. He came to understand that it wasn't kids who don't love their dads who were kidnapped and thrown to the dogs, but uncles who love their nephews.

Many years later, on the day he took out the photo album that his mother had managed to save at the cost of a few pistol whips from the Special Forces, his eye was struck by a black-and-white shot of his uncle: Sertac sitting on his lap, looking directly at the camera with a serious, scowling expression, not smiling despite all the exhortations of the photographer. He remembered the day his uncle showed him a picture of his beloved and asked him, isn't she beautiful? And though her plump lips and the beauty mark to the left of her delicate nose caught his attention, he hadn't been able in that instant to say anything to his uncle; with a thousand and one regrets he closed the album.

The question at hand truly was the question of *Love and Revolution*. His uncle was, according to rumors, a member of a *Maoist* Kurdish faction, and, completely unbeknownst to Mao lying in his tomb, and to all of Communist China, for that matter, he was killed by some traitor, for freedom and future, on one luckless winter day.

So that's how it was, and they would make fun of the revolutionaries. People like Sertac's paternal uncle and his dimwit wife completely disregarded the revolutionaries, took no heed of their ideologies. They would say Uncle Mihemed was, like Sertac himself, dumb as rocks; they would say Uncle Mihemed was a bit of a hopeless romantic and had thrown away his life chasing pie in the sky.

It was the time of black bags and white collars.

It was the age of *Alî gel* and *Alî koş*.

Alî was always and ever *gel*-ing and *koş*-ing on the blackboard.

And Sertac was always in pursuit, with his huge, black eyes.

* * *

At any rate, his teacher was not like his uncle. In fact, nobody at his school bore any resemblance to Uncle Mihemed. Whenever the fatheaded, potbellied teacher saw the kids from the Lower Quarter misbehaving or heard them swearing, he would twist their ears with his dirty fingernails before starting to kick and slap them.

He would humiliate those kids in the middle of class, bust their balls to entertain the fine-faced, fine-smelling kids of the colonizers. Because they always had their fingers up their noses. Because they stole snacks from the Upper Quarter kids. Because Sertac picked a booger from his nose and rolled it *squidge squidge* into a ball the size of a lentil and stuck it on the bottom of his desk. He obviously saw Sertac do it, not once, not twice, but many times. One day, almost out of the blue, the teacher stood over him, asking him what he was doing. Not wanting to answer, Sertac began crying to distract from the question. Unfazed by those tears, which were nothing but a lazy plea for mercy, the teacher went to the front of the room and announced to everyone: "Excuse me, class, your friend Sertac is rolling his boogers into little balls and sticking them under his desk." Of course, everyone erupted, *eeeeeeek* and *ahahahahaha*. In fact, a number of the girls immediately asked for permission to go to the restroom. In the end, most of his classmates began avoiding him, refusing to draw near or interact with him for some time. But, like many things forgotten all too quickly, such as natural disasters and acts of God, Sertac's booger balls vanished from memory in no time at all. He was growing up.

But *Alî* remained as he'd always been, constantly *koş*-ing and continually *gel*-ing without growing so much as a millimeter. Sertac, on the other hand, was growing; a long time had passed since he quit picking his nose. He had left so many things in the past. These days what drew his attention was the blossoming shapes of the girls' bodies.

* * *

The moment he felt the urge, he'd run home and lock himself in the bathroom. That business—yes, he was engaged in precisely that business—began consuming every moment of every day like a duty given to him by God above. This was his second discovery: masturbation.* He imagined that the stuff he shot out of himself was his brain and was afraid one day he might end up without any brain whatsoever. His brain would dance on the surface of the water for a bit before vanishing down the drain, and he would swear at himself, "Man, fuck my brain!"

His mom, in the meantime, was overjoyed by how much time he was spending in the shower, believing Sertac must be taking fastidious care to wash every nook and cranny, scrubbing his body with wool fibers till his skin was red. "Cleanliness is next to godliness," she found herself repeating; she'd knock on the bathroom door and ask him if he had enough hot water. But neither the hot water nor the terebinth soap was enough. He had other demands to make of this life. The fine-faced, fine-smelling girls at school had brainwashed him with their lips, mouths, chins, breasts, and nipples, and they simply wouldn't leave him alone. He could not get out of his head the image of two fire-hot bodies that he cut out of a naughty magazine, which he lost because he left it in the pocket of his only pair of pants when they went through the wash; and so he lied to his weary, hapless self.

No longer did he tell others, "I'm a doctor." The kid who wore pajamas *tatterdemalion* and *elasticwaisted* and *tigerstriped*,

* Masturbation is the act of erotic self-defilement, a sin in the eyes of God and, quite frankly, in the eyes of both this author and this translator. (Trans.)

tight as hell and *stinking* of poverty, hand-me-downs from uncles and cousins, finally came down from his hiding spot on the roof, not that there was any longer a hiding place to speak of. For those terrible idolaters came and wove their web of destruction, laying waste to everything. Sertac remembered how his father was in those days, fearfully babbling a mile a minute to his mother; they were talking about fleeing, and then, and then:

about tonight,
about books,
about Uncle Mihemed and his boots,
about the kids,
about the attacks the other night,
about killing and dying . . .

They spoke in a whisper, spoke of how so many people from Zerdav had been taken away, of how they were being delivered into the hands of the *Gods of Fear*. This was his third discovery: fear. He feared his father would be arrested, he feared he would die, he feared soldiers, all their bluster and all their guns, their uniforms—everything about them, even their shadows.

But like all students made to be obedient, in time he too carried the flag, joined in all the ritual celebrations of national holidays, marched in lockstep at all the national parades and demonstrations, had pronounced as loud as he could, *How happy is he who calls himself a Turk!** But for the love of God, why didn't he feel the slightest bit *happy*?

* Attributed conventionally to Ataturk, this phrase has long been a popular nationalist slogan and was the final line of the pledge of allegiance for many decades. In its poverty, the Turkish language has no grammatical

* * *

Gone were the days of self-gratification. Even though his mother had admonished him at home, "We're Turks"—saying it in Kurdish no less—and even though his teachers at school proclaimed in Turkish that *the Turk has no friend but a Turk,** something still wasn't clicking for Sertac. There was a terrible hollowness to all these proclamations, but he couldn't figure out what it was. At five after nine every November 10, the very minute on the very day that Ataturk died, he and his classmates would stand motionless and soaked in the rain, and his teachers would yell, "Cry already, you little brats! Shed those tears for Ataturk!" and he would wonder what the hell they might do if he didn't. Some of the other students truly did begin to cry, at which point others would make fun of them; but when the whole ritual was over, they would return to their classrooms together, freezing to death. Right then the members of the *Teachers' Council* would raid the classroom, one of them guarding the door while the others wandered the room like wolves through a flock of sheep, beating the living daylights out of the Lower Quarter kids with canes and metal rulers until they finally did shed those tears. It was in that state that the

---

gender, nor even gender pronouns, and so the phrase could equally refer to a nationalist of any gender. (Trans.)

* Consider, by contrast, the well-worn saying, albeit of unknown provenance, that "the Kurds have no friends but the mountains," a phrase beloved by well-meaning Westerners like myself who want to draw attention to the historical, and ongoing, and, in fact, unending plight of the Kurds. (Trans.)

teachers would then make them recite those national anthems of this most modern civilization. Yes, the third thing he discovered was fear: an intense fear, a savage fear, a heart-stopping fear. He wasn't one of them, it seemed, or he *was* one of them but not one of them *enough*; he had so many shortcomings, but eventually, ever so slowly, those shortcomings would be allayed, *ever so slowly*.

* * *

Yes, Sertac was growing up, and his love was growing up too, nourished by poetry about love and lovers. He would hold her hand and lead her beyond the baleful boundaries of the school grounds and find refuge in the shade of a tree among the young people of the Upper Quarter. But no matter how many times he kissed her hands there, or told her, "You belong to me," she wouldn't dignify him with a response. Whereas the kids of the Lower Quarter would say, "Shame on Sertac for dating the daughter of a cop!" to which he'd reply, "You're just jealous!"

She was a beautiful girl, Merasîm, a sweet girl. She was tall, with a narrow waist. She had dirty-blonde hair and blue eyes. At one point, Sertac found an excuse to bring her to his house. His mom adored Merasîm, treating the girl like she'd descended from on high, finding her flawless as she watched her movements, awestruck exactly as Sertac was. Merasîm was the family's only daughter; her dad really was a police officer, a Kurdish police officer, and though she'd been born with a silver spoon in her mouth, she wasn't as stuck up as her peers. On the way to his house, Sertac explained to her his family's situation. "We're really not well-off, economically speaking. We don't have a couch, and our TV is still black-and-white." He continued to dig himself deeper into that hole. "We still sit on the floor to eat, and I don't have anything like a room of my own." He really wouldn't shut up. "My mom can speak with you in your language, but she's not very good at it." And he apologized to Merasîm. But Merasîm smiled back, and Sertac wanted Merasîm to always be smiling.

"My dad asked for a change of station."

"What, really?"

"We're leaving, Sertac."

"No, come on!"

"We're leaving."

"If it's because of the attacks, I can stop them."

"What? How?"

"With love."

"In your dreams."

"You're my only dream."

"We're leaving, Sertac."

And she wept in Sertac's arms like she had never wept before. Three months later, Merasîm vanished. She had taken her beautiful blue eyes with her, and Sertac's death was just around the corner. The only thing he hadn't decided was where or how he'd commit suicide. Even his suicide note was ready. The letter was in the pocket of the single pair of pants he owned, and it wouldn't be ruined when they went through the wash. Because Sertac was growing, and as he grew up in Zerdav, so too did death; menacing diatribes reverberated from the speakers on the mosques' minarets every single day. The young men of the Lower Quarter were gathered into military formation in the courtyard of the municipal building, *left, left, left right left!* And the corpses of the martyred guerrillas were lined up side by side under the camellia tree for everyone to see. Who would have the temerity to say anything about that? On the march back all of Zerdav's dumbasses would whisper to one another.

"They look like animals from Africa."

"Snakes, they're snakes!"

"They're scorpions, they stung themselves!"

"Was that so-and-so's son?"

"Didn't that look like what's-his-name's daughter?"

"She wasn't wearing underwear."

"Good Lord."

Some officer stood on a chair and addressed them all. "Look closely now! Look closely at all of them! They defied our state, defied our army, and you see what happened to them as a consequence. Warn your kids, don't let them join these terrorists, these Armenians, these Bolsheviks, these hoodlums, these cum stains."

After the officer's speech the bootlicking mayor chimed in with a few brownnosing words of his own. The young men of the Lower Quarter sang some Turkish anthem in reply:

> "This nation, acclaimed in history for its humanity
> The republic's dream, our Ata's legacy"*

They were not allowed to stop until they got to the gate of the school, and they spent their lesson that day watching these untended corpses. That night, Sertac didn't sleep a wink. He was still looking for his Merasîm, but he didn't know why.

* One of the more vapid anthems in the Turkish nationalist repertoire, so lyrically and musically repugnant it's not even worth naming here. (Trans.)

* * *

After Merasîm left, Sertac drowned in that whole jaundiced autumn. The worst part of it all was how everything everywhere looked yellow as an egg yolk. Any person, any place, any thing he turned his eyes upon, all he saw was yellow.

What a filthy yellow!

What a repulsive yellow!

The yellow of death!

He never so much as touched his spoon to the yellow rice they served every day at lunchtime. The yellow tea they gave him at breakfast never passed his lips. His father's eyes were getting yellower and yellower by the day. The same was true of the glass in the windows he opened to smoke cigarettes. The pair of black shoes he gave to Hiso the Bootblack returned to him as a yellow pair of shoes. Things were really no different with their black-and-white TV. In the evening, the whole family would gather round, watching segments of corpses being dragged behind armored vehicles, half-heartedly clicking their tongues the whole time. The blood had lost its color; it became in the TV glow a sickly yellow that washed over them. Many of the people he knew had gone with their families to coastal cities, which were like visions of paradise. Still others caught their breath in Europe. Those left behind in their penury bought yellow canvas from Nedîm the Clothier and had Sefer the Carpenter use it to upholster yellow coffins. When he finally finished school, Sertac was a completely yellow person. His mother no doubt thought he looked yellow too, jaundiced. Rumor had it that Sertac was sick, but if you asked him, all the birds of the bourgeoisie had fallen ill. "The fear of a red revolution filled our hearts, so we got stuck with yellow," he'd say. His friends would simply reply, "You're just afraid of dying."

They couldn't convince one another. They'd stay up reading *the reddest of red* books till the middle of the night and still not understanding a thing. One of his friends swore on his mother's life that there was no bourgeoisie in Zerdav. "Government employees and their families are all bourgeois," another would insist.

They would go on and on until Sertac's father would set the *Book of the Lord* down before them and say, "Here you go—this book contains the answers to all your questions. If you're real revolutionaries you'll read the Qur'an."

At that they'd all run for their lives, fleeing his house like a bomb had been tossed into their midst. They'd yell from afar, "Your dad is the very embodiment of a comprador!" To which he'd reply, "Fuck you, Menshevik fags!"

Pîra NAH kept clicking her tongue, though he could never quite figure out where that sound was coming from. But she was there, Pîra NAH, her ear turned to listen to those fools.

* * *

Sertac's paternal uncle and his dimwit wife sat in the living room, letting the fan blow on them as they clacked their prayer beads. Sertac moped his way through the room without greeting them and went into the kitchen amid their *tsk tsk*s, their murmurs, and their clacking beads. Full of anger, Sertac opened the refrigerator and cast his eyes over its contents. He took a pitcher he thought was full of lemonade and lifted it up to guzzle it down. It had barely crossed his lips when he spit it back into the pitcher.

"Dude, what is this?"

"What's what?" It was his father's voice.

"What's this in the pitcher?"

"It's holy water from Zamzam. You didn't drink it, did you?"

This story was his story.

9

HE REALLY IS stupid. If he hadn't been so stupid, his wife would be by his side right now. Their last fight had broken out because Sertac had closed the door to his office, or, more accurately, his jackoffice; that door stood open right now and had not been closed since Merasîm left, which was really when everything came to an end. Plagued by these thoughts, Teacher Sertac enters this room; he doesn't really have it in him to do any work, especially in here, so he takes a book off his shelf in a way Merasîm would have hated and looks first at the cover before flipping through the pages and then returning it to the shelf. Not a single part of him wants to wipe down the old, shabby desk, to inspect the various sundries on the desk and change their places over and over again, no, and least of all, to sit down and write. What is there for him to write about after this, except for the thrashing his heart and his mind have undergone? He is afraid already, deathly afraid, of losing his mind, of going fully off his rocker. Right as he leaves the room his eyes land on the Qur'an that Alî Osman had given him as a gift. Why the

Qur'an, instead of another book? He hadn't asked, of course, but he told Alî Osman, "I've done my ablutions," as he took the book, even though he hadn't, at which the boy's eyes glittered. "Don't do anything like this again," he said, "giving me gifts and all that, especially at school." It's on the top shelf now, and he goes and stares up at it with some hesitation, wonders whether he should leaf through it or not, but he hasn't done his ablutions and so he doesn't know what to do. He jumps as though something invisible has passed in front of him; he is overcome with goose bumps. And in that instant, a fear overtakes him. He swears against *The Devil*, casts Him out, and then casts himself out onto the balcony. He needs to hear noise now, needs life, needs to hear the many sounds of living around him. He needs to hear the sounds of children, of animals, of cars, to find comfort in the listening.

10

EVERYTHING THAT BELONGED to him was there.

In that room.

In his jackoffice.

Virtually everything.

All the way back to his foggy past.

Which was also in the old, shabby desk.

The desk his father gave him.

Hoping for a calm, argument-free night, Sertac Karan aka Antique Sertac entered into his chambers at the early-evening hour of six thirty, carrying with him the gray comforter he stole from his military service and a cup of bitter, tar-black coffee, and around the time his "wife," Merasîm, was supposed to arrive he locked the door, turning the key in the lock twice with a resentment he harbored from the previous night.

Exactly two times.

Click and *click*!

If he could, of course, he'd *click* two locks onto Merasîm's tongue.

Just two little *clicks*.

That night, with the air of a steadfast believer, he raised his hands toward the heavens in a grand, theatrical gesture, his eyes fixated on some corner of the ceiling, which kept him from taking the whole affair too seriously. And with a trembling, weak voice—and invisible ceremony—he beseeched God to use *His Divine String* to tie shut Merasîm's jaw.

Exactly two times.

Click and *click*!

Because the thing that Merasîm hated more than anything else, that made her go ballistic with vengeful rancor, was the fact that he would not stop locking the door to this room. It had happened most recently just three days earlier, and when she realized it, she tried to throttle him; she jumped down his throat, every word in her tirade more vulgar than the last, until finally she dragged him out of the room.

"Have you lost your goddamned mind?" she said. "Did they feed you donkey brains or something? Have I not told you a hundred and twenty times that this door must must must not be closed? Why do you keep locking yourself in there? Like there's anyone apart from the two of us living in this house? Unless there is and nobody's decided to tell me? Tell me who are they? Who and what are you hiding yourself from, you idiot?"

Buoyed by three Turkish words, *bireyci*, *asosyal*, and *soyutlanma*,* that had lodged themselves like contagion, like tumors, in their shared vocabulary, her insults and her threats and her

* *Bireyci*, individualist; *asosyal*, asocial; *soyutlanma*, abstraction: Merasîm may as well be diagnosing the ills of capitalism rather than those of her poor, unfortunate husband. (Trans.)

reproach became the topic of their nightly conversations, in the form of her psychological analysis of his behavior.

All night long . . .

All the same roles, all the same expressions: Sertac looked pitiful in the yellow, half-dead light that infected the bedroom furniture and infected their words with malaise, and Merasîm kept talking all the while.

"No, nobody should marry men like you. Seeing as you love being alone so much, why'd you trick me into living here? You got tired of me and of marriage too quickly, Sertaco! Was this what we agreed to? You're hurting me, but you're hurting yourself too. Look me in the eye and tell me, why did you say, 'I love you and I will love you till death do us part'? Why? You think you're such a great, irreplaceable guy, that there's no man above you, is that right? Who do you think you are, you bastard? No, I don't know you. The Sertac Karan I knew is dead to me. Where has he gone? I'll say it one last time: That door is not to be closed, and that's final!"[9]

In that instant, Sertac Karan aka Masochist Sertac would have wanted to cry.

In that instant, Sertac Karan aka Nothing-at-all Sertac would have desired to shed his tears, which were entirely sincere.

In that instant, Sertac Karan aka Prior Sertac would have wished to rest his head on the lap of his mother, may God rest her soul.

In that instant, Sertac Karan aka Yes-of-course-yes Sertac would have thought about using bullets to splatter his beloved Merasîm's brain all over the wall.

Exactly two times.

Pop and *pop*!

* * *

Husband and wife would sometimes go days in the same house, even in the same room, without speaking. Each of them, especially on long winter nights, would sit in opposite corners of the living room, without making eye contact, without making conversation, spending hours in silence staring at the television, and when the romantic comedy they watched into the early hours of the morning was about to end with its familiar outcome—a happy ending for the happy couple—Merasîm would resentfully press the *off* button on the remote, darkening the screen, while Sertac would turn off the lamp, and with sleepy eyes and long yawns he'd follow close behind his wife into the bedroom, which would bring him back to life.

Merasîm would fall asleep right away, taking as much distance as she could from her oppressive home life as fast as she could. She'd turn her back to Sertac right when she got into bed, and soon after pulling the heavy quilt farther onto her side of the bed than was her due, she'd find herself on the other side of slumber until dawn broke, though she did occasionally talk in her sleep, and Sertac, ever the insomniac, paid close heed to this, her subconscious, trying to find some key word, some phrase, some hidden name over which he could agonize and interrogate her the following day for the sake of opening the door onto a brand-new fight.

The fights . . .

The fights between Merasîm and Sertac . . .[10]

It was a routine thing for them, the fighting.

Like sleeping, waking, washing their faces and brushing their teeth, or like eating, getting dressed, and walking, fighting became an indelible part of their everyday lives. Merasîm was, at any rate, always ready and willing to cut off her nose to spite her face. Whenever something was brought into the house without her permission or against her wishes—Sertac would do it simply to push her buttons, pouring money down the drain solely to spite her, buying teacups, aluminum dishes and spoons, decorative saltshakers and ashtrays, cheap pots and pans, regardless of whether they needed them or not, and bringing them home in a state of unparalleled and self-satisfied agitation—she would raise hell and scream at Sertac, her shrieks resounding Earth and sky.

"You're insane! You're insane! You're insane! You're insane! You're insane! You're insane! You're insane! You're insane! You're insane! You're insane! You're insane! You're insane!"[11]

It used to be that their fights came to physical blows; she'd drag him to the bedroom as soon as she got hold of him. And after who knows how many dozens of never-before-heard combinations of insults and swears, never-before-conceived curses and damnations, after so many broken belongings and strewn-apart rooms, husband and wife would find themselves rough-and-tumble in their marital bed.

Then Merasîm would turn her back, burning as it was, to Sertac.

Then Sertac Karan aka Amorous Sertac would wrap his arms around her and first kiss then bite her sweat-drenched neck.

Then they would enter the threshold of some gentle, bare-naked slumber.

Then they would sleep until they awoke and warmed each other up again.

Exactly two times.

* * *

Once upon a time they laughed *hah hahah hahah* at the marriages of their friends and families, even though these marriages were mostly *hahahah hahah hah* loving happy marriages; but before the first year of their own marriage was up, it had been destroyed, quite like a sandcastle, by the very first signs of troubled waters. They no longer slept together; Merasîm took the bedroom—probably because it was closer to their cluttered wardrobe—while Sertac sometimes slept in the living room and sometimes in his jackoffice.[12] Ultimately, their hearts grew colder much as the air outside did, and even though they couldn't heat their home because the new landlord—a traffic cop—was a stingy bastard, the story was, at least for Sertac, not yet over.[13]

Although it did not snow as much that year as everyone expected, the ardor of winter was nonetheless greater than usual, as if the lack of snow was caused by the sins of man—especially men like Sertac—as if the weather had meant to cause a storm but simply gave up, as if it couldn't bring itself to go all the way, like some of the wimpier seasons, and opted to vent its frustrations with wind, with rain, with sleet and hail. This, too, was a kind of vengeance, though, and this winter, like last year and the year before, the indigent of the city fell to feuding, for there was no coal available to them. The angry revolutionaries said it all happened because it turned out that some sacks of coal distributed in the Lower Quarter were filled—no joke—with dirt and dust, while others were full of manure. Truly! All the children and grandchildren in the Quarter were wretched, overcome with sickness and cough due to the cold and the lack of medicine. They had neither fantasies about what they would do in the warmth of a coal fire nor language to communicate their adversity to the Upper Quarter. This despite the fact that the Upper was no farther than the width of a coal stove away from the Lower Quarter. In short, the revolution had not yet arrived, and even though the word *revolution* and its watered-down meanings disgusted Sertac, perhaps because he was tired of how watered-down that word had become, how contagious its problems were, when the Lower Quarter came up the only thing that came to Sertac Karan aka Sertac Aforementioned's mind was his sobs in the throes of death.

* * *

Sertac Karan aka Single-room Sertac only felt good, only felt like he had distance from his problems, in this single room of his, which must have been because his darling Merasîm was not sleeping in this room, or else was keeping herself busy with cakes or pastries or other baking projects that warranted far too much work. At such times he'd enter into his jackoffice like he was stepping into a holy temple, with all the requisite veneration and solemnity, and before he took a seat in his black leather chair he would examine the bookshelf, which contained mostly works in Kurdish.

"There's still something missing," he'd say. He said the same thing to himself every time he cast his eyes on his shelves, before collapsing into his black leather chair and delving into his half-baked story, its outcome unknown.

* * *

Everything that belonged to him was there, in this room, much of it on the old, shabby desk that Merasîm had cursed hundreds of times over, rightly or wrongly—perhaps because of the weight of the thing. Notwithstanding its three rather voluminous drawers, the desk was such a sullen object, it was reminiscent of both him and his father, and it did nothing to stimulate his creativity. Once the desk entered his jackoffice it lost any allure it once had, but because his father swore up and down it was very old, an antique even, it had to be cherished dutifully. And now, although he regretted bringing it into his home, he couldn't bring himself to pawn it off to the antiques dealer or, better yet, to throw it in the trash and be completely rid of it, at least while his old man was still alive. Even though such a thing would not just be unpleasant but impossible, Sertac Karan aka Obsessive Sertac nonetheless puzzled at great length over various schemes that would rid him of that creature known as his desk, which seemed otherwise quite content occupying half of the entire room. He puzzled and puzzled over it: one, hire a junk collector; two, move the desk himself, in the cold with a thousand and one obstacles, not just out of the office but also out the front door; three, lift it onto the junk collector's back and, as if that weren't enough, help him carry it down; four, run into Merasîm on the way out and have no choice but to explain the situation; five, subject himself to her humiliation and opprobrium; six, let her embarrass him and bust his balls over and over and over without objection; and seven, after debasing himself for the world to see, leave that junk collector with the desk and run away with tears in his eyes. No, it just wasn't possible! The desk weighed on him, but he didn't know what he could do without disappointing either his wife or his father. Sertac Karan aka Lump-in-his-throat Sertac could not help but curse his misfortune seven times over, curse the old-fashioned complaisance that always hung over his head, which Merasîm had twice already hit him upside. Though he hadn't said a word about Merasîm hitting him upside the head to his "unmanly" friends, they knew as soon as they saw him that Merasîm had gotten hold of him and had, as usual, knocked his lights out. They even had a bet going among them about "how" or "with what" Merasîm had hit Sertac upside the head.

"It was an ashtray!"

"It was a pitcher!"

"No, a vase, it was a vase!"

"It had to have been a picture frame!"

"A mirror!"

Sertac Karan aka One-of-the-guys Sertac hadn't been able to restrain himself, and lashed out at Silêman the Pinko-poet.

"I swear to God, you are no friends of mine! If you were my real friends, if you loved me as much as I love you, you wouldn't have left me alone at my wedding only to say, a few months later, 'Let us stop by when you're free, so we can give our regards to the happy couple.' Is that what friendship means to you, Silêman? Is that what comradeship means to you? Hmm? Answer me, asshole! How soon you managed to forget, you dick! Yes, how soon indeed. Man, don't you remember when I hid you in my house for days on end? You fucked all those girls up the ass in my house, you made a mess of my perfectly clean comforter. Don't you remember pissing all over my bathroom? You, sitting there looking the way you do, you're gonna make fun of me?"

The friends whispered to one another.

"Hand to God, I can't think of a stronger man than Merasîm."

Then they cackled.

But in the end, Sertac and Merasîm got married, and after that scandal of a wedding—Merasîm's old friend Sergîno was possessed by who knows what to pour an entire bottle of vodka all over herself *glug glug glug glug* and then light the lighter *in a flare*, throwing herself around like a fireball, chanting insane slogans and roaring like a bear all the while—his friends set about getting married too, sending their parents, their kith and kin, to make the necessary arrangements, having their own merry wedding parties complete with the wedding band, the drum and clarinet, and then buying their own homes, thereby saving themselves from the humiliation of renting. But how, by what means, would they escape the watchful eyes of their wives? Wives who acted like the guards in the *panopticons* that *Jeremy Bentham* described, not allowing their husbands, full-grown men, to even go to the bathroom without their permission. Sertac would laugh his ass off.

"Hah, hah, hah, haaaa! Ha, really, ha!"

And whenever Sertac would run into his friends' wives, he'd sour his face like he was laying eyes on his father's would-be murderer and would look away; never mind shaking their hands, he wouldn't even say hello to them.

"Them and their wives who are a hundred times more dimwitted than them, fuck them!"

None of those wives had anything even close to an original idea about what was happening in the world, in the city, even in their immediate vicinity, nor did they have a sense of any of their own problems; all they did was hold their husbands' hands and churn out babies. Not just one, not just two, not three, not four, *amen amen amen amen*! And no sooner would they have gotten home with their little bundles of joy than the wives' breasts would start to sag, and they wouldn't want to fuck, and the men would start sleeping with those one-off wives who sold themselves, before returning on Fridays like wingless angels, and in that brief moment as they did their ablutions *glug glug glug glug* they would talk of honor, especially women's honor, and of revolution. And Sertac would interject angrily, interrupting their ablutions.

"All the men at the whorehouse are talking of revolution!"

* * *

Sertac Karan aka Bat Sertac may have sought refuge in his jack-office, hoping for a calm, quiet night, but he feels more helpless, more exhausted, more worn down than he did yesterday or the day before, owing to the chaos in his head, which keeps making his brain throb with pain and thereby prevents him from working on his unfinished story, from adding to it or taking things out, as a result of which he hates both himself and the state he's ended up in. It had been him, hadn't it, him alone? Hadn't it been him, one hellish summer day fifteen years ago, returning to this raucous, upside-down city, only to lose his mind in a home filled with his nightmares? Had he not come of his own free will and full of hope, only to be stuck there, unwilling and hopeless? Had he not wanted to pursue his sacred profession by other means? He had gotten married, settled into a home, and started working as a postman when less than a month later they cut him off without any rhyme or reason, right? It had indeed been none other than him, Sertac Karan! But why was he always doing this to himself? Cloistered away in his jackoffice, he would smoke and smoke and smoke, lighting a new cigarette with the butt of the last as he ruminated for hours on end. Most of the time, without knowing why, he would not be able to sleep until dawn broke. For reasons unbeknownst to him, he would often come to his office as soon as his wife drifted off to sleep. Because when he stayed there, he would drift into sleep until a nightmare triggered by something he didn't know—always the same nightmare, to be fair: Merasîm becoming a famous author with his stories and returning from another one of her award ceremonies with her friend Sergîno, who would pour a bottle of vodka all over his desk and then set it aflame—jolted him awake.

So, he had sought refuge in his office earlier in the evening, hoping for a calm, quiet night, wanting to continue on with the story, just the story! For this story was his story, and this was how it began: "One hellish summer day, fifteen years ago . . ."

11

THE BALCONY WAS filthy with neglect, a layer of dust and dirt over everything, and the railings, which could no longer be considered white, were covered in sparrow shit. No, this isn't how it was, this isn't how it used to be, no! Everything used to be squeaky-clean; the apartment used to always smell fresh as daisies. Even down to the curtains in his office; Merasîm washed them once a month, though it was, of course, his job to hang them up. Every time he ascended the fold-up stepladder, which played a major role in accomplishing many of the chores in the house, and attempted in a kind of odd battle to hang the curtains, his head would spin, he would whine, and he would curse the man who invented curtains a hundred times over.

Teacher Sertac is thinking; he is thinking about night, he is thinking about sleep, he is thinking about how one might manage to sleep without nightmares. Should he plug his ears with wax, to protect himself from the voice of Pîra NAH? No, he will turn up the volume on the TV, all the lights will of course already be on, and he will do the best he can not to see himself in that cursed mirror. Perhaps he will sleep in his office, rather than his bedroom; in so doing, he will have reduced the distance between himself and the kitchen.

12

"YEAH, YOU GOT that right, brother," his uncle said—*clack clack clack clack*—to his father—*clack clack clack clack*—as he swilled his milky coffee—*clack clack clack clack*.

"He doesn't get along with anyone."—*clack clack clack clack*—"I've been trying to tell you all day! No respect for his elders," —*clack clack clack clack*—"nor for God nor the Prophet."—*clack clack clack clack*—"He doesn't abide by our customs or manners," —*clack clack clack clack*—"so he decided the night before Eid" —*clack clack clack clack*—"to go to the village. Good Lord! I told him a thousand times not to go; the villagers'll recognize you, I told him, they'll give you up right away."—*clack clack clack clack*—"But no, I may as well have been talking to a wall."—*clack clack clack clack*—"It goes in one ear and out the other."—*clack clack clack clack*—"And in the end he did what he said he would and left in the dark all on his own."—*clack clack clack clack*—And Sertac went and asked his uncle to count his prayer beads more quietly.

"Stop flicking your tizbî so loud!"

The sound had so irritated Sertac that he felt himself on the verge of doing something unspeakably evil. He trembled; his face flushed red with anger. He hadn't yet said everything he wanted to say, when the excruciating ache in his head was exacerbated by the feeling of his father's five fingers on his left cheek. He hadn't taken that possibility into account, God have mercy, no! The sucker punch knocked him over, made him see stars. And while Sertac's uncle tried to restrain his father with *no*s and *don't*s, Sertac yelled out as he ran to the kitchen and returned with a knife; but his uncle's dim-witted wife snuck up behind him and brought down an ash shovel as hard as she could over and over on his back. "Oh God," she exclaimed, and Sertac collapsed to the ground with shrieks loud enough to pierce flesh, and his mother, who still loved Nizam more than him, also started screaming.

"You killed my son, you gangly bitch!"

So that's how they do it, then: They attack men from behind, women do, with treachery. After that day Sertac never saw his uncle nor his dim-witted aunt again. Yet his uncle and his dim-witted aunt embarked on a vicious campaign of propaganda against him, going so far as to report him to the district governor's office.

Pîra NAH perched on the languid branches of the fig tree in front of their home like an owl, hooting and hooting over it all. Sertac could feel her, could feel that something bad was going to happen to him. As that feeling overtook him, he fell silent, and a shudder began in his fingertips and passed through his whole body.

* * *

Sertac made up his mind: He wouldn't leave the house for a few days. Whatever bad thing he expected to happen would likely befall him outside somewhere, which was why he decided not to leave the house whatsoever, not even to go into the yard. What a dreadful situation. Sertac's exhaustive and exhausting paranoia prevented him from dreaming as his heart desired, from eating and drinking whatever he wanted, from sleeping or from spending too long in the bathroom, from reading, from keeping himself busy with anything, from doing everything and anything at all.

He didn't know what *normal* people did in situations like this, but they surely didn't do what he was doing; they couldn't imprison themselves at home, they couldn't give up eating and drinking.

Fear, it was fear!

It was fear that put him in these states.

Fear of being caught.

Fear of *death*.

Fear of every last shitty thing in Zerdav.

He knew there were secret agents waiting at the ready to put him away and willing to spite themselves to do so, and so he tried to console himself.

"I'm the child of a government clerk; they can't do a thing to me. They can't just come up and lay their hands on me, and besides, it's not like I've done anything anyway."

So spoke Sertac, though he wasn't sure his claim was exactly true. Because they had gone and interrogated a friend of his: who's this guy Sertac, what's his business, who's it with, what's he do, and so on and so forth. And that idiot, regardless of who he was, even if he meant to protect Sertac, would probably have said, "*Brother*, Sertac might be a member of *Dev-Sol* . . ."*

It totally upset the applecart. The secret agents, he was sure, were already up his ass from morning till night. The call, in other words, was coming from inside the house. They sat in front of the shops and made idle chatter with the shopkeepers. Sometimes they'd buy things on credit. "Guess they don't make enough money," Sertac would say to himself. That's how it seemed to him, at any rate. They'd go down to the market and try to rip off the steadfast greengrocers over tomatoes, over peppers, over eggplants and potatoes. They'd have wives and kids too, and they'd have family picnics and hold hands. They'd get sick as well, and go to the doctor. It made Sertac wonder, how was it that these men, these agents of violence in the world who wreak torture with their own two hands, could look anyone in the eye? How was it that they could greet people, say hello, smile with the grace of God? That was what wracked his brain, even though he hadn't yet been arrested, hadn't sat through an interrogation, hadn't yet faced torture or been thrown in prison. He knew, in theory, how cruel those sons of bitches were, he had read about it, and since he knew about all the unspeakable things they do to a man who won't talk, Sertac knew he didn't want to fall into their hands. He didn't want to stand around naked with them as his audience. He didn't want them to shove

* So what if *Dev-Sol* aka *Devrimci Sol*, the predominantly Turkish *Revolutionary Left*, assassinated multiple high-ranking members in the Turkish military and intelligence apparatuses? So what if they also assassinated American military personnel? So what if they're a quote-unquote terrorist organization? Let he who is without sin cast the first stone. (Trans.)

their truncheons up his ass and then make him lick their truncheons clean. He didn't want them to bring his parents in and do unspeakable things to them in order to get him to confess. Nor did he want them to electrocute his armpits, his fingertips, his fingernails, his balls, or his dick.

"Those guys," Sertac told himself, "are no different than *car mechanics*.[*] They have the same tools of the trade: pliers, clamps, screwdrivers, nuts and bolts, wire and cable, irons and rods, hammers and nails, rubber and forceps. The social theory of implements and devices, the art and craft of torture, the flawless aesthetics of it all, the boundless hatred, an animus that has survived since time immemorial, an animus against humanity itself. Sure, fine, but why do they have to do it like that? If only they'd put a bullet in our heads and save us all the time that torture takes!"

It was easy to say, and so Sertac had decided: He wouldn't leave the house!

* * *

He was utterly besieged by fear. That was, in fact, his cruelest torture, what he inflicted upon himself. Staying was torture, waiting was torture, every second was torture. Not a soul heard his voice, nor did anyone come to his aid. All of Zerdav ignored him, the son of an infidel bitch! He sat at home, in a completely empty room, staring at the wall, with the hope that some door, some portal of light would suddenly open up and pull him into a

* All mechanics are crooks. Not a one will see the gates of Heaven. (Trans.)

different world. A place where the word *torture* wasn't found in any dictionary. Was there such a place? Could there be? A place where people weren't fucked by truncheons. A place where electricity was used not for the business of torture but for the illumination of dark streets. A place where pliers and clamps, wires and cables were forbidden. A place where there were no screams, where all you heard were the moans of people making love. But where was that place, that utopia?

* * *

When someone—or someones—began pounding on his door, the fear coursed through him. "They've come for me," he said to himself, and indeed, they had come for him. He was all alone and he had already made preparations for his departure the previous night. Everything except his white tennis shoes by the door was more or less where it belonged. Looking at his ID for the umpteenth time, he recollected something his father had always told him.

"Bring your ID with you everywhere, even when you go to the bathroom."

They had come for him; they had come to bust down the door. In that instant, what was it he felt?

Fear?

Grief?

Anxiety?

Emptiness?

They had come and they had at least saved him from the waiting. The trembling in his fingertips ascended to his brain.

He couldn't remember the exact moment he reached for the doorknob. The door opened suddenly, and all at once he was surrounded by armed executioners, face-to-face with pistols and rifles and the guy who informed on him. There were nine or ten people in total: a few of them outside, a few in the doorway, a few in the yard. The informant was the only one without a gun. They had dressed him in military fatigues and blindfolded him with a black cloth. Sertac approached the informant; a single word came out of his mouth. "Why?"

The informant looked so pathetic, flanked on either side by enormous special ops troops. He couldn't see anyone, but he could hear the insults those motherfuckers rained down on Sertac, on his parents. They clung tight to his arms to keep him from fleeing, to keep him from hurting them, himself, or Sertac. Would it have been possible for the informant to do anything in that situation? There was no trace of a beating on his face; his lips were simply chapped with thirst. The laces of his *Mekaps*,* which

* Let's say you're the CEO of a shoe company in the 1970s. You've just launched the Mekap, an innovative work shoe that is the first of its kind to be produced in Turkey, intended to compete with and replace demand for foreign alternatives. Imagine your shoes sell like hotcakes: affordable and durable, "ovens for your feet," as the ads say, good for all conditions. Imagine, a decade later, that your Mekaps are so successful they become the standard-issue shoe for the Kurdistan Workers' Party, a pair given to each new guerrilla who enlists—Mekaps to traverse the rough mountain terrains in all seasons and weather conditions. Let's say your Mekaps come to signify, in the words of the Kurdish anthropologist Dilar Dirik, "the guerrillas' abdication of life under the capitalist system, as well as a selfless dedication to the cause of an oppressed people's liberation."

Let's say, then, that the Prime Minister of Turkey derides that insurgency—one of your most reliable purchasers—by saying that the were covered in the mud of Zerdav and Zerdav's villages, had been removed. They had dragged him over hill and dale, leaving no village or town unturned. Now he was here, at Sertac's door, trembling, his head hanging sadly, lacking shoelaces. The special operatives had lugged him by either arm the distance from his home to the Zerdav Police Headquarters. In the end they slapped cuffs on Sertac's wrists and dragged him to the station as well, threatening, beating, and belittling him the whole way.

Pîra NAH[14] came and landed on his left shoulder and spoke to him.

"As for the *Companions Of The Left*, they will be Damned . . ."[*]

This story was his story, and it was still to his left.

---

guerrillas are no more than "a handful of youth hiking in the mountains, wearing their Mekaps." Imagine that people start referring to your shoes as "shoes for terrorists," and the police detain people for selling them or even wearing them. Let's say your shoes continue selling like hotcakes nonetheless, and that after nearly four decades of market success, of reliable purchasing by Kurdish guerrillas and their supporters, your Mekaps have become a beloved symbol to millions of people, something they brandish at protests, something as symbolically dense as a keffiyeh. If your "only crime is producing a quality good," and you've made a killing doing so, then you would be a fool to write — as the CEO of the Mekap shoe company did — to the Prime Minister of Turkey and tell him that "If it would put an end to terrorism for us to stop producing these shoes, we want you to know that we will do so without any hesitation."

That, dear reader, is not just the story of Mekaps—that is also the absurd scourge of nationalism and, more importantly, that is dialectics in motion. (Trans.)

* And over them shall be sealed vaults of Fire from which there is no exit. (Trans.)

13

THINKING ABOUT HOW things have turned out, about the disaster that has befallen him, about the Qur'an in his jackoffice, Teacher Sertac is thoroughly perplexed. What would he have done if that Qur'an weren't there, if it didn't exist at all? What did he used to do? What had he done? By what means had the Qur'an conquered his heart and soul and taken his breath away? Was that what filled him with fear? Hoping to rid himself of these thoughts, to overcome his fear and save himself from its dead ends, its ebb and its flow, so that he could spend the whole night without worrying, he returned to his office and took hold of the Qur'an. He held it with deep reverence and kissed it three times; his eyes filled with tears as he thought to himself, "I don't even know what you contain! And I don't get how you can fuck with me and my soul so much when I don't even believe in you! I don't know."

* * *

What dream?

Sertac Karan aka Dogmatic Sertac opened his eyes very suddenly, after which he lay very still, trying to figure out where he was, until he realized that he was in his jackoffice, awaking from a strange dream. The gray comforter pilfered from his military service had fallen on the floor, and his saliva had thoroughly soaked a patch of it. He was shivering and yet he couldn't bring himself to lean down and grab the comforter.

In this dream, he had wandered far away from his office, far, far away. He was in some other room with Merasîm; she was holding his folder of stories—unfinished stories—and she seemed to be speaking as though presenting at some international conference, as though she were joined onstage by a number of renowned critics and commentators before an audience of eager spectators, sure of herself, of her criticisms and comments, chiming in with occasional asides on her personal life, her marital problems, and her relationship with Sertac. Sertac Karan aka Unfinished-story Sertac longed for the sweet, darling Merasîm he had seen in his dream.

Why did he wake up now?

Who or what wrenched him from this dream?

He looked at the clock on his desk: five minutes till seven thirty, and Merasîm still wasn't home. Or perhaps she was home, perhaps she realized his office door was locked again, and instead of kicking it in opted to wash her hands of him altogether, going into their cold bedroom to change her clothes instead. And after that? No doubt she would come into his office. No, she would have to surmount his barricade, which is to say the door; she would do so by saying, in a voice that was not harsh, "Open the door," and Sertac Karan aka Solid-doored Sertac would not make her have to repeat herself; still under the influence of his dream, he would get up from his desk and open the door for Merasîm, leave it open to her forever. Forever and ever . . .

Before long he heard, through the locked door, the giggling and voices of unfamiliar women. Someone said Sertac's name. It must be someone asking how he is. Upon hearing his name, the malaise that had accumulated inside him dissolved. It had been some months now since anyone other than the porter, their cheapskate of a landlord, and a couple of impertinent beggars had come knocking or stopped by to visit. If anyone made the mistake of visiting, they wouldn't stay for too long, put off as they were by Merasîm's words and actions and especially by the bitter scowl that clung to her face; they would get up and with a thousand apologies head straight home. Which was why Sertac Karan aka Inglorious Sertac asked a few people in his closest circles to keep their distance for a while and to not ask the reason why. The reason, however, was clear: Merasîm didn't want to see her husband's bosom buddies around the house.

"There's no need!"

In that instant, Sertac Karan aka Taking-it-personally Sertac wanted to run away from home as soon as he could.

In that instant, Sertac Karan aka Dark-future Sertac wanted to join the guerrillas at the peak of one of the proud and thankless mountains.

In that instant, Sertac Karan aka Creator Sertac wanted to re-create himself.

In that instant, Sertac Karan aka Fallen-asleep Sertac wanted to accompany a wounded crane in flight.

* * *

Three of Merasîm's girlfriends had come, three girls who'd given up almost all semblance of shame, three girls who didn't concern him in the slightest, three girls who planned to stay the night. Sertac Karan aka Submarine Sertac offered them the briefest welcome from the doorway of his office, and after excusing himself for the important matters he had to attend to, he locked the office door exactly twice and stood over his father's antique desk. Merasîm hadn't even looked at him; she just went straight to the kitchen, carrying three overstuffed plastic bags.

It was excitement that Sertac Karan aka Gone-bust Sertac felt. He sat down in his black leather chair, and, filled with the inspiration that so rarely struck, he picked up his pen and wrote a single word in the middle of a sheet of paper, which was the exact moment he realized he would never, never, never finish his story. He finally realized that this life of his, this life devoid of any meaning at all, only emerged as the outcome of these unfinished stories he never, absolutely never, ever, experienced himself—he was the product of one of those unfinished stories. He babbled to himself. "No. No, I'm not going to concern myself with the cause. I'm not going to let myself be dragged down by the things ruining my life. Nor am I going to blame anyone either. Not because I'm oppressed and these tribulations befall me and make me ramble on like this, no. And it's not just people; I'm not going to blame my circumstances either. This is my truth. The roar of the fighter jets must have turned my brain to mush, must have shredded the last few images I can remember from my childhood and youth, must have messed with my mind. Or maybe I really and truly am a madman. I knew a madman once. He would enter the courtyard of the mosque by our house every morning and just stare and stare at the minaret before crying out, 'God, you are great! God, you are great!'

"And after his screeching and beseeching he'd start laughing strangely; little nuggets of shit would fall out of the hems of his pants, which were too short for him, and piss—his piss was dark—would soak through his pants, and when the imam finally set out to beat him with sticks and stones, he'd begin with his lamentations. I watched everything from my window and felt bad for him. Now, though, I speak with the same words as that madman. 'God, you are great! God, you are great!'

"I know myself, I alone know 'what' I am. No, I was never 'somebody.' They kept me from becoming somebody; they didn't even let me see myself as a normal person. Do you know what I am, Merasîm? I am an unintended outcome, the outcome of experiments that could only have been conducted in a colonial laboratory."

* * *

Sertac Karan aka His-very-own-accomplice Sertac kept talking to himself until the new day dawned. He occasionally raised his voice, but nobody, including his wife, took any interest in what he was saying; not even the visitors asked Merasîm why her husband was acting the way he was. Roused by the morning call to prayer, he got up and went to the door, and after turning the key to the left exactly twice, he crept quietly to the toilet, careful not to make any noise. All the doors in the house were closed; he couldn't be sure who was sleeping in the bedroom and who in the living room. The kitchen had been tidied; the plates had been washed and fastidiously laid out to dry on the marble counter. Spoons, knives, forks, water glasses and tea-cups, all in order. The stove had been thoroughly wiped down too, given that it shone bright. A plate of dessert awaited him in the refrigerator, a relic of the ladies' revelry, but he didn't feel like eating it. He sized it up and it sized him up back. It was a strange scene: this bitter life of his, this sweet leftover dessert. Bitterness devoured sweetness and sent him back to his office, leaving a sour taste in his mouth.

PART TWO
Doubt

14

THE FIRST TINY flakes of snow begin silently collecting on the tips of the weeping rosewood tree's branches in that godforsaken garden, and Sertac, Codename Revolution, looks out with teary eyes from behind the fogged glass, beholding the scene, which briefly mollifies him with an ill-timed and ill-starred—for was he not ill-starred!—warmth; enraged as he is, he wants to bang his keffiyeh-less and doubt-filled head against the window and scream, but no, it isn't possible; believing in the revolution keeps him from paying any heed to, or feeling any shame over, all those things that pass through his mind and his heart without his intention, or even his permission, but mandates instead that he let them all fall down on him like the snowflakes outside, that he sit by the window rather than put up with how annoying all the riffraff around him was, all the asses, the idiots, and the slackers crowded into that musty room; and yet, with all the petit bourgeois feelings he feels toward that pitiful, faded rosewood tree, those tiny little bourgeois feelings petit as petit can be that fill his mind and his heart, he wants to cry, cry out, clamor and scream and shout for himself and for all the wretched of the Earth.[15] Who knows, perhaps this half desire had caressed his mind several hours before the snow started, in one of the brief moments of madness that had taken his mind in that room whose door seldom opened. The brief moment gives him goose bumps.

What was madness?

What was it like?

What were its symptoms?

For example: Did it ache?

Like love? Ah, love!

Seated in front of the window, Sertac Karan aka Vagabond Revolution wants to smoke a cigarette, and with his jittery hands he tries to flick the lighter, but he can't, it has no gas, so he throws it hard against the wall. Filled with his anger, Sertac Karan aka Out-of-gas Revolution leaves the room.

Leaves the room?

When did it become *his* room?

Who said this room is yours, told you to look after the room?

Nobody!

Nobody has said any such thing because he has made no such demand.

How would he have?

And of whom?

Yes, of whom?

His head echoes with the words of that traitor, that son of a rat bastard, Rojhat the Army-man. "You'll see in time, dear

Brother Revolution, because no matter how easy or difficult life as a revolutionary can be, it will save you completely from all the afflictions you had before you joined. Right now, in my eyes you are afflicted, you're sick, man, sick!"

He was sick.

He was sick with a sickness the name of which was unknown to him.

What did he have?

What was he sick with?

What was it that steered him, and people like him, away from the path of a shattered, tasteless life, and so strenuously toward the path of the revolution? Had it not been his own very personal decision to join up?

"Revolution is the water of life. It is medicinal, like an IV at the hospital, for instance, the way the IV enters your blood drop by drop. I'm telling you, Brother Revolution, it's not like tossing back a pill and swallowing it down with a glass of water, no, you get a little of it bit by bit, until it's all gone."

And now it was all gone.

Because that IV, that dark, sickly sweet IV, that revolution still hadn't even begun when they started injecting it into his veins on the godforsaken day he joined up. It finally arrived to his heart as a poison one evening after three entirely wasted years, when, after having dutifully carried out the task of writing his daily report, and as he prepared to write a letter to his mom, his dad, his sister, and his brother, Codename Revolution saw the face of that son of a rat bastard Rojhat the Army-man suddenly appear in his room, arriving with a piece of terrible news, which he delivered like tidings from Heaven.

"Revolution, my dear brother, please accept my condolences for, your sister, Canan."

But Codename Revolution would not accept those condolences, nor would he be condoled of her sicknesses, which that whore-spawn Rojhat the Army-man called "the sicknesses of the petit bourgeoisie."

"What was she sick with, Brother Revolution?"

So, she killed herself? Poor thing. And with poison, rat poison no less? By her own hand? She lived in a house full of cats, and rumor has it, she took her life in the middle of the night. It wasn't a dream. Sertac Karan aka Utterly-dazed Revolution learned the details from his comrades over the course of a few days. Pressing a photograph of her brother, Sertac, along with his first and last letters, to her chest, she left the world behind—haunted by memories of her older brother, who left one bright spring day three years earlier, stepping out of the dark-yellow door of their ramshackle house under the guise of going to buy bread and apples.

It had been a departure without return.

That final letter, folded in seven, reached Canan by way of their cousin Aziz after several months of pain, sorrow, rage, and longing had passed. Sertac Karan aka Steel-willed Revolution explained, in brief, his decision to enlist in the struggle, his sudden disappearance, his justifications, how things were going—in a manner that would reflect well, of course—and ended it by saying: "I have become a tool of the revolution now, so do not wait for me, for I will not return until my homeland is freed."

* * *

With a sullen voice Sertac sounds out Canan's name a few times. He hasn't woken up yet; he's still asleep, still in the middle of a heartbreaking dream while lunch preparations are underway with a strange rush and nervousness in the other room. It is the middle of the day, and from afar the *high*s and the *ho*s and the *high-ho*s of their toiling are accompanied by the clatter of cups and spoons and aluminum dishes, which resound in his dreams. In their hurry to serve the pasta left to cool outside, the too-salty stew, and the bland, rubbery rye bread, nobody comes to check on him, as if they mean to say nobody cares about him, their friend and comrade and brother; nobody parts the curtain on his dreams to stir him from the sheer boundlessness of his slumber. This time too, he will lose his mind, as has happened many times before, without "intraorganizational" or "revolutionary" support, without the voice of a mother or sister or lover rushing to his aid, speaking to him in a voice that calls to mind the melody of a sweet song, and all the brawls and the toil and moil and the self-defense and the self-control and the strife and struggle will intensify as his dream draws to a close, and though they would usually shake him awake or pour a glass of cold water on his head to bring him back from the brink, to stop his heart from bursting, this time he will wake up suddenly and all alone. Sertac Karan aka Fiercely-nightmared Revolution will call out to Canan from his dreams, he will beg her not to commit suicide, he will implore her not to kill herself, he will cry out, will weep, will howl like a dog, but he will not be able to make his voice heard, and Canan will not hear her older brother's voice, she will not even turn to look; she will merely knock back the whole bowl of poison like it's a shot. Sounds will come from far away: the meowing of cats harried by hunger, the clatter of cups and spoons and aluminum dishes, the *oohs* and *ahs* of orgasms, the varied pitter-pattering of shoes and flip-flopping of slippers. It will be his turn to clear the tables, and Sertac Karan aka Lazy Revolution will still be fast asleep.

* * *

"I don't have a sister named Canan," Sertac Karan aka Sure-of-himself Revolution says to Rojhat the Army-man. "You obviously got hold of bad information about me," he continues. "But even if I did and she took her life with rat poison, I wouldn't look at it the way you do. It's less your callousness than your fear, a secret fear." He pauses, waiting to observe the effect his words will have on Rojhat the Army-man, who is busy twiddling his mustache, anxiously chewing on its ends; he is defeated, as he had been yesterday, and the day before, and the day before that. Sertac Karan aka Tactical Revolution has checked his opponent's king with a bishop, a rook, and his queen when Rojhat the Army-man makes an unexpected riposte, slamming his fist down on the chessboard and scattering the pieces. He glares threateningly at Sertac Karan aka Careless Revolution from his seat. "Nobody can defeat me! You European partisans, you know nothing but idle banter! What fear, man?" He pauses briefly before calling out to his beady-eyed ass-dragging bean-head of a guard. "Dijwar!" Dijwar staggers into the room and greets his furious ranking officer with a nervousness so practiced it's comical. "Yes, Commander Rojhat!" Rojhat the Army-man tells him to pick up the chess pieces on the ground and put them away and then to go and ask Seyîd Elî for the car; there is important business to attend to at the Committee. "He will go," says Sertac Karan aka Smart-as-a-whip Revolution. "He will go to the comrades who are just like him, and he will beg and plead."

* * *

Neither rain nor snow.

Clear weather.

Bright-blue skies.

Sertac Karan aka Skipped-his-lunch Revolution snacks on a couple of things before going into his jackoffice and locking the door twice, *click click*.

Exactly two times.

Click and *click*!

What does the room even have to offer him, though? What is it that draws him into his office and keeps him in there for hours, for days on end?

"Perhaps it is something about the office itself," says Sertac Karan aka Office-bound Revolution.

"Or maybe it's the feeling that comes with being in here," says Sertac Karan aka Lover-of-possibility Revolution.

"How nice it feels to be in an office," says Sertac Karan aka Asocial Revolution. And so he sits down in his wooden chair to pass the next several hours with the idlest of tasks, like glancing over sheafs of paper, or experimenting with different kinds of ink in different pens, or looking through magnifying glasses of various sizes, or studying the etymology of some old Kurdish word.[16]

* * *

Neither rain nor snow.

Clear weather.

Bright-blue skies.

Sertac Karan aka Detective Revolution begins to think about the bygone days of his jackoffice. Who lived here before they rented the place and moved in overnight, before the uprisings, before the city was turned upside down? Which military officer, which state official, which traitor? What kinds of things had been done in this room? What specifically happened, specifically in this room? Murder? Rape? Abuse? General immorality? The nail holes in the wall catch his attention.

Were there photographs here?

Photographs of what, of whom?

Of animals?

Of girls?

Of generals?

Of religious icons?

Of revolution?

Sertac Karan aka Dubious Revolution pauses on the word "revolution"—or rather, he gets hung up on the word. Why did they give this to him as a code name? Why didn't they ask if he would be content with a name so grand? Does he really not like his name? Even if he doesn't, what can he do about it?

A few things are written in Arabic script on the wall to the right of the desk; the sentence—if indeed it is a sentence—isn't very long, but the handwriting is beautiful.* Sertac Karan aka In-danger Revolution picks up one of his magnifying glasses and sets himself to examining the writing.

* * *

"Stop! Stop right there. Which Canan is this Canan? Who is she, why haven't you told me about her?" Merasîm interjects, and with her hands still busy kneading dough in a big bowl, she shoots a completely unrelated request at a totally bewildered Sertac. "Come here and add another cup of water to the dough, chop-chop!" Sertac Karan aka Bucket-head Sertac looks helplessly and pitifully back at Merasîm, who is, after all, in charge of everything, and stammers out a reply. "I... didn't... finish... the story... yet." Merasîm retorts admonishingly, "Dude, I'm asking you about Canan! It better not be that dumb cunt Canan, you know the one, she had her eyes on you? The fugly one?" Merasîm had not been without reason in calling her "fugly," thereby calling attention

* *In the beginning*, the story goes, *was the Word, and the Word was with God.* But what was the Word? Why did God guard it so closely? Perhaps that was why they built the Tower of Babel in the first place, wanting to know the Word that God kept so safe and so close by his side; how beautiful the Word must be, they thought, and in those days of universal language they would have been able to understand it. It is written in the hadith that once the Tower was completed and King Nimrod of Şînar ascended it in his belligerent hubris, he looked upon God and shit himself ["voided his excrements"], and so God confused our languages. Thus was born the profession of translation. (Trans.)

to her own beauty and using it as a cattle brand on the heart of Sertac Karan aka Helpless Sertac, who had once taken an interest in fugly Canan—rumor had it—out of *boredom*. "No," he replies. "For God's sake, what made you think of that Canan now? The name came to me from the novel I was telling you about." "Yeah, right," Merasîm says, shaking her head, as if to ask, "Who do you think you're kidding?" Sertac Karan aka Let-his-guard-down Sertac grabs a cup of water. "I wish it were acid," he thinks to himself as he pours it on his wife's hands still kneading the dough in the bowl. "Whatever, man, I wanted you to say something about the plot of the story, but I guess you're busy. Don't think you'll be making much of that dough, though. I'm starving!"

"Eat my shit!" Merasîm shouts. "Get the fuck out of my sight!"

* * *

Neither rain nor snow.

Clear weather.

Bright-blue skies.

Sertac Karan aka Prevaricating Revolution wants to understand what the Arabic written on the wall means and why it is not written in a line but at a downward slant. Because if it were merely text, he wouldn't be giving himself a headache trying to decipher it.* If it were merely text, he would have called someone

* *In the beginning*, I thought I could make easy work of this text; like every self-respecting translator, I would have taken my time, assiduous in the word-by-word toil and moil of translation, committed in my imbecilic curiosity to the veneer of understanding. In the beginning I had faith in my fidelity, trust in my mastery, but I did not know—could not have

who understands the Qur'an to come translate it for him. If it were merely text . . . But no, Sertac Karan aka Fastidious Revolution realizes that there is something else beneath the text; it is a human face drawn with the same writing implement. Yes, yes, it is human.

But why?

Why so beautiful, and beneath the text?

What is its connection to the text?

What if there isn't one?

Sertac Karan aka Magnifying Revolution picks up another magnifying glass and places it atop the one already in his hand, trying to see the text, the face, even more clearly, to make out its details and understand what the whole thing is about. And he figures it out—it is a masterfully drawn anatomy of the human body.

But why is it drawn on the wall?

And not on paper?

Who drew it?

Why?

The picture is embellished from top to bottom—and left to right; all over, really—with Arabic letters.

What do these letters mean to say?

What do they describe?

If only he knew!

---

known—how the text would slant, would bend, would betray my faith, would master me. I am unmade. I am awestruck and I am fucked up. And so I will no longer posit myself as master of this text. I will no longer lay bricks to rebuild the Tower of Babel. I will no longer be a foot soldier in the battle for prelapsarian language. I refuse to be a guard in this translational panopticon, I refuse to be a warden in the prison house of words, and I refuse to be the nimrod shitting himself at the top of his tower. (Trans.)

If only he knew what they said.

If only he knew who left them there.

If only he knew why they were inscribed on the wall.

If only he could solve the mystery of why they're there on the wall.

Sertac Karan aka Finely-sifted-tightly-woven Revolution begins finely sifting through his memories, and his mind becomes a beehive buzzing with questions and possibilities. He does not know why he is toiling over the details of *this* text instead of the texts that guide the revolution. For what purpose could he be letting himself languish over it?

But why is it there?

And why does he fly into a rage at Rojhat the Army-man and others like him?

"Because of his actions," says Sertac Karan aka Lost-the-taste-for Revolution to himself.

"Because of his mockery and insults," says Sertac Karan aka Allegedly Revolution.

"Because of his weird boastfulness and arrogance," says Sertac Karan aka Failed-revolution Revolution.

Most of all, because he regarded himself as a talented, courageous, cunning commander who lords over the rest of them. He considered himself the best, the most revolutionary, among them. The belt on Rojhat the Army-man's waist was longer and certainly more expensive than the one that belonged to Sertac Karan aka Short-belted Revolution. Rojhat the Army-man was one of the old guard. He had been in so many skirmishes over the years, had been cooked in the fire of revolution; one day, a stray bullet ricocheted and lodged itself in his left shoulder, and that bullet wound became cause for his pride and vainglory, became a story that Rojhat the Army-man told and retold. He had managed to win over so many people to the struggle by doing so. He was a member of the *Political School*, and so showing him the utmost respect was a sine qua non. Soon he would bring his wife here and they would rent a house together, for he had earned the right to a big, spacious home.

That was Rojhat the Army-man.

* * *

Sertac Karan aka Beating-himself-up Revolution regretted nothing, neither the decision he made to enlist nor how his life was on the base. For some time now, though, he'd been having occasional nightmares. For some time now, he would wake up near noon and stay up till the following morning in his room, spending all night goofing off with medical textbooks and with the pictures in them, preparing his reports, playing with sheets of Letraset, looking through magnifying glasses, watching the avalanche of bugs emerge in the dark, observing the maneuvers of spiders and scorpions and solifuges, translating, contemplating, dwelling on memories and daydreams.

For some time now, he has been finding solace in a fantasy about one of the village girls. He is dying for her. Thanks to her, he is coming back to life.

One morning at dawn, she leaves home with a pitcher in hand and over by the henhouse she squats down and pisses *piddle piddle piddle* and then with the water in the pitcher she washes *squelch squelch squelch* her crotch. It is winter. There is snow on the ground.

A wild steam rises up from where she pissed, and Sertac Karan aka Freezing-his-ass-off Revolution watches in secret and at length from behind his curtain as it all happens.

"This must be why the revolutionary struggle has encountered setbacks," Sertac Karan aka Intellectual Revolution supposes in his heart of hearts. "Out of an abundance of time. I have so much time. We have so much time. We spend twenty-four hours of the day in the camp; we've seen neither mountain nor valley, neither cave nor pass, neither grove nor field, neither shortcut nor long way, neither slope nor wreckage; not a single thorn has pierced our bodies, nor has a single one of us come face-to-face with a bear; we've neither heard the babbling of a brook nor gotten a sunburn on the breast of the mountains . . ." So he pontificates to himself before returning to the text, or picture, drawn on the wall.

* * *

One day Codename Revolution and Rojhat the Army-man got in a fight over his room. Someone—he knew sure as the wind blows who it was and what their ends were—had entered the room under the pretext of cleaning it up. They had intended to get hold of something he had supposedly written about Rojhat the Army-man; they rifled through everything, from his drawers and bags and boxes to between his books and notebooks, underneath and even on top of his bed, all the way down to the pockets in his jeans, turning over the whole room like the police would, hoping to find some evidence, some rat poison or an exploding cigarette, a chemical lighter or anthrax paper, any sign, even just a note from which they might be able to extrapolate, to uncover his grand and flawless plot to murder Rojhat the Army-man. But, quite naturally, in the course of their paranoid pursuit they came upon nothing. Sertac Karan aka Critical Revolution was remarkably calm as he spoke to Rojhat the Army-man. "Up till now I haven't taken a single life, Uncle Rojhat, and I won't either . . . goddamn it! The day before yesterday I accidentally murdered a praying mantis. It was her fault; she raised her sawlike arms and waged a savage assault on me. When I used my magnifying glass to look at her, I had no intention of killing her, I swear to God I didn't. She misunderstood me, lost her mind, but I lost mine even more, and because of that fear I brought my box cutter down on her. Her head flew off and rolled away, and a fluid that was somehow both dark and white oozed out of the bug's ass. I was just realizing what I'd done when . . ." Rojhat the Army-man stares back at Sertac Karan aka Lost-his-mind Revolution, as if to ask, "What the fuck are you talking about?" and he leaves without saying another word. Sertac Karan aka Praying-mantis Revolution realizes that the writing and pictures on the wall have been vandalized with a dagger that does not belong to Celadet.*

* Celadet Alî Bedirxan: the man who devised a Latinate alphabet for Kurdish and wrote a story called *Gazinda Xencera Min* (Reproach from My Dagger). In the story, the narrator is being scolded by his dagger for its lack of use. Having become a writer, the narrator has foregone violent struggle, advocating instead for the war of national liberation to be waged in words. "Qedrê min bizane," the dagger admonishes, "ji min dûr mekeve, min ji xwe dûr meêxe û bi min ne qelema xwe, lê parsûwên dijminên xwe jêke!"—"Know my worth, do not turn from me, do not leave me behind, and do not sharpen your pencil with me, but stab me in your enemy's rib!" The story ends as a parable about the pen being mightier than the sword, but honestly, I'm with the dagger on this one. (Trans.)

15

DOUBTLESS THE STRANGEST and most colorful patient of psychiatrist Dr. Sarîn Zavaryan, Sertac Karan aka Beyond-hope Sertac, arrived, as usual, an hour before his final psychotherapy appointment, sullen-faced in the early-morning hour that filled *normal* people with the hope that motivated them to lead pleasant lives, and he waited to be called by the secretary with the juicy ass, whose sexy movements and flirtatious looks made his mouth water. That lovely spring morning, Sertac aka That-lovely-spring-morning Sertac appeared to busy himself once again with the faded, yellowed pages of the old psychiatry magazine, struggling courageously to control his wandering eyes, trying not to look where he shouldn't, especially not at the pale white legs he saw reflected in the tile below the desk. He had read most of the articles in the magazine dozens of times—most of them were about the wretchedness of schizophrenia*—and he had memorized the titles of the articles and their authors' names. Taking the magazine into his hands for the very last time, he turned right to the article by Dr. Sarîn Zavaryan—he knew it word for word—which discussed in great detail his illness, as well as her methods of treatment. It gave him a balmy, prodigious feeling of hope. Despite the many efforts and entreaties of that Armenian siren—Dr. Sarîn had called a few of her colleagues after their third session to ask for their help—Sertac Karan aka Thick-headed-and-also-stubborn Sertac hadn't responded to the treatment at all. He was in his head, where he left no stone unturned. As he saw it, this was his story.

"Yes, there was a country called Kurdistan, and it was in the country's largest city, the ancient city of Amed, that he came into this world. Amed was the rose of Kurdistan; it was a mighty poem, a steadfast will, a proud past, before it splintered into shards, *alif lam mim* . . .

"He had a patriotic mother and father, well-read and discerning. His mother's name was Zarşîrîn, sweet tongued—she had been a famous ballerina in her youth—and his father was named Mîro, though they called him Doctor Mîro—he was a

* *A Thousand Plateaus* sounds to me like the title of a Turkish nationalist screed—look up the so-called Celestial Turks, a favorite fetish of Turkish nationalist primitivism, if you dare—but Deleuze and Guattari really nailed the whole schizophrenia thing: "People say, 'After all, schizophrenics have a mother and a father, don't they?' Sorry, no, none as such. They only have a desert with tribes inhabiting it, a full body clinging with multiplicities . . ." (Deleuze and Guattari, trans. Brian Massumi, 1987: 30). (Trans.)

doctor of philosophy, in fact; they were not actually named Zekîye and Fethî.

"He had two sisters—Hevok and Kevok—and two younger brothers—Serdest and Kawa—all named for folkloric heroes and all following in their parents' footsteps. His name wasn't Sertac at any rate, and those who called him Sertac were doing him a great disservice. His name, the name that his father gave him, was *Ferheng*. Ferheng was a Kurdish name; it meant dictionary, and it suited him quite well.

"At his father's command, on the day he was born, before he'd even left the delivery room, a famous Kurdish lexicographer whispered two hundred *feminine* words into the baby's right ear and two hundred *masculine* words into his left. With his father's encouragement, he began writing short stories when he was twenty-four, in his mother tongue, of course; he had no idea where the notion that he had started at forty came from.

"A great wrong had been done to him. Ninety percent of the charges against him and his life were lies, no more than fabrications and baseless gossip. The one who debased him with her wiles, who had nothing to do with her life except to scheme against him, who laid traps at his feet day after day to make him fall, was none other than—may her cunning be her downfall!—his uncle's wife, that dim-witted hag, wasn't it? Yes, it was her!

"He only now realized what had been happening. How could a naive psychiatrist, especially a woman, have any idea what was going on? No, it wasn't possible that the truth would come out through these sessions, through modern therapeutic methods, and through who knows how many painkillers and computer reports. How could it be possible?

"What do you mean, Sertac? What do you mean, Karan? His name is Ferheng—that's that! He was born in Amed to a patriotic family; at twenty-four he became a writer; he was single; he had no wife named 'Merasîm,' and they had neither a wedding nor connubial bliss.

"Hevok aka Canan, she committed suicide in the shower with rat poison. When did there start being so many rats? And the cats, are they just sitting around? *Alif lam mim* . . .

"Was Serdest, who bragged about the meaning of his name, really oppressed? And Kawa, he went off and joined the puniest, most worthless faction of the Kurdish movement, and he got himself killed in cold blood, didn't he? Who was his murderer? And why?

"His name is Ferheng and he was born in Amed, the largest Kurdish city, not in Münster, Germany. He has never and will never see Münster in his life.

"Oh please, there's no city called Amed, are you kidding? And Kevok, why didn't Kevok ever marry?

"In that case, your patient Ferheng—or, as you put it, Sertac Karan aka Patient Sertac—is experiencing a series of fantasies removed from reality, as if in a dream; he is experiencing incidents unrelated to the realities of his havoc-run homeland as though they're stories that haven't yet been written down. None of it is true! So, Ferheng never emerged from that mouthed, tongued cave. So, Ferheng, or, as you put it, Sertac Karan aka Shameless Sertac, suffers from disorganized schizophrenia and has not responded to any treatment.

"I don't understand whom you think you're explaining this to. You know that the person sitting before you is not Sertac

Karan aka Carefree Sertac. And you know that no schizophrenic could ever make up—much less experience—so many dozens of stories, images, tales, and scenarios, except with the help of a fatheaded, wide-eyed, three-fingered alien. I'm sorry, but I don't believe you, even though you say you're a psychiatrist, and psychiatrists don't lie to their patients—I wonder—still, still, how should I put it?"

* * *

Sertac Karan aka Romantic Sertac was a sensitive man. That Saturday morning, he had rushed out of his house on an empty stomach in order to get a gift for Dr. Sarîn, who had for some time now adorned his suddenly sticky dreams. He walked all the way from the Lower Quarter to the market in the Upper Quarter. On his way he'd fantasized; now he was a fearless Kurdish militant, a bravehearted revolutionary. He had been tasked with some delivery by the Committee, apparently; this time, his task would be difficult, he must remain vigilant, mustn't approach any of the towering walls that surround the military buildings filling the city top to bottom, mustn't make simple mistakes and give himself away. According to the scenario, what he was to deliver was a stack of forbidden magazines, and Dr. Sarîn was awaiting him and the magazines at the safe house.

He was in good spirits. Now he would win Dr. Sarîn's favor, would be someone important; Dr. Sarîn would look at him differently, because now he was a fearless Kurdish militant, a bravehearted guerrilla, Codename Revolution. As soon as she saw him, Dr. Sarîn would embrace him; no, first they would discuss ignorance and the state of society, and then, after their conversation, Dr. Sarîn would praise his manner of speaking, his word choice, his bravery and intellect and even his Che-like mustache and beard, and she would give him her hands, which would be trembling beyond her control. Dr. Sarîn would give herself up to his nimble fingers, and he would make that beautiful Armenian gazelle moan with his blasphemous pounding until she said "gi pave!"—Armenian for "enough!" And the Committee, appalled at what they did in the safe house, would put a bullet in both of their heads. No, no, together they would stand before the committee leader and confess their love, after which . . .

Sertac Karan aka Artist Sertac hadn't been able that morning to come up with a happy ending for his fantasy, and so the joy he'd felt moments before was replaced in an instant by dark clouds of sorrow. Now he was no longer a fearless Kurdish militant, a bravehearted revolutionary; the truth had caught up with him, deaf pilgrim, in the form of a car going a hundred and twenty through the city's single intersection, blaring its horn at him.

Who was he?

Who was Sertac Karan aka Unrecognizable Sertac?

Why should a woman like Dr. Sarîn give her heart to a sick person?

Was there a dearth of men?

Who was Ferheng?

Why did the traffic cop stare straight at him? The guy must've suspected something; something strange, something not going according to plan. He'd been sweating his ass off, had waved from the middle of the road a few times like a maniac. Where did that drooling dimwit know him from? In any case, he was no longer Dr. Sarîn's beloved, he wasn't carrying illegal magazines or anything; he had nothing except his expired ID, a little bit of money, and sweat.

When he arrived at the turn to the Upper Quarter, his knees were giving out beneath him from his panicked running; his tongue stuck to the roof of his mouth, and he was panting heavily. He slowed down as he passed the Army Enlistment Office and walked along the left edge of the narrow sidewalk; at the security gate, as many as twenty to twenty-five sunburnt young men stood, looking with a strange sense of urgency for their names on lists posted behind glass-covered panels; it must be their time to go off on their military service.

He reminisced about his own military service. One day, out of nowhere, a yellow envelope was placed in his hands and they spirited him off to some Central Anatolian city. He completed his eight months of service without even using his ten days' leave; it had been a screeching nightmare. Eight months, yes, eight months away from humanity. Because as soon as he saw any "humanity," he'd rub one out of his engorged and burning tool onto the disgusting, graffiti-covered walls of a bathroom stall. He got himself off at least four or five times a week, using only spit. Got himself off... Not because he was horny, no, but because he was suffocatingly and hopelessly bored all the time.

He was hungry and his stomach ached, but he hesitated to go to a restaurant and eat his fill. The place he always went to was on the way; right now, though, it was doubling as an aid organization collecting supplies for the Palestinian people. The

Arabophiles of the city must have lost their minds again over the Palestinians, even as they turned a deaf ear to the suffering of their own people, and Sertac Karan aka Of-Kurdish-descent Sertac didn't want to go and tear them a new one first thing in the morning.

Sertac Karan aka The-vengeful-spirit-of-Angra-Mainyu Sertac had decided: From this moment forth, he would not support any deceitful, one-sided internationalism, even by eating a meal; he would turn away from God, who only worked for men of the cloth, and dedicate himself to the evil way of Angra Mainyu. Zarathushtra was waiting for him.

Deep in these thoughts, he crossed the street, wanting to get to his friend's bookstore as soon as possible. They had run into each other a few days earlier, in a square in the Upper Quarter; Zarathushtra had told him that some new books had arrived and invited him to the shop. "Thanks, Zarathushtra," he'd replied, unable to forgo courtesy, "perhaps another day." And they had parted ways. As is widely known, the most meaningful gift is a book, and on that beautiful spring morning, Sertac Karan aka Thick-booked Sertac was going to buy a book for someone who'd given him no hope for love.

* * *

Sertac Karan aka Dour Sertac finished Dr. Zavaryan's article in the magazine, and when he lifted his head and looked unintentionally at the desk and saw the secretary overcome by the romance novel in her hands, he, too, was overcome. "Would you look at that," he muttered to himself. That juicy-assed woman had taken out the romance novel on purpose, he realized, had spread her snow-white legs on purpose, had wanted nothing more than to show him the curly blonde ringlets on either side of her lacy red underwear.

What was left of his mind was consumed by that view, and he didn't know what to do, couldn't figure out what idiotic thing to say to her. He coughed a few times, unable to restrain himself and wanting her to compose herself already, and asked for a tissue in a weak, trembling voice, so that he could wipe the sweat off his wide, heavy brow. And like she'd been waiting for this very request, she put down the book in her hands—without marking her place, just closing it—and opened her purse with an excitement that gave herself away, handing him a tissue and offering to bring him a cup of water. After apologizing softly for her distractedness, wearing a shit-eating grin that suited her so well, she retreated to her corner—and to the previous order of things—and that's where the movie was interrupted.

In her office, Dr. Sarîn listened to his "historic"—his word—and "final" objections for exactly two and a half hours, a serious and attentive expression on her face, as Sertac Karan aka Fantastical Sertac transmogrified before her very eyes, at turns becoming Ferheng cloistered away in the mighty mountains, or becoming the world's most hopeless man jumping off those mountains to the ground below. He poured his heart out to Dr. Sarîn.

"It was one o'clock when I arrived today. I came right on time, neither late nor early, and stood before the secretary's desk at exactly one o'clock, and she—like you—was expecting me.

"I did not look at her with ill intentions, nor did she shake her tail at me. By God, she welcomed me with a warm smile, directed me right to your office without a single question.

"I did not see her lacy red underwear or anything, nor her snow-white legs. She wore a long-sleeved undershirt and ironed black pants, as well as a headscarf.

"I did not look at the psychiatry magazine to read your article, nor did she read a romance novel.

"Like I said, I was here exactly at one o'clock.

"Yes, yes, I didn't leave home before eleven; I was fighting with my parents. At eleven thirty I left the house, terribly angry, seething with rage. I cursed the villagers. I cursed how far I've fallen. I arrived here by finding empathy for the minibus drivers.

"In fact, I wanted to get you a gift, but I decided against it so you wouldn't misunderstand me. The way your boyfriend the teacher looks at you, it rubs me the wrong way. I'm sorry, I'm sure I'm overstepping. I've heard stories of patients falling in love with their doctors, but what could be more beautiful than being direct and honest? While I do not have such feelings toward you, when I see you I am overcome with endless happiness—it sends me soaring, and it's all because of your sincere candor. The dialogue you've forged with me isn't of the ordinary kind between any old doctor and his or her patient; it is something more, because, surely, you've already come to realize I am no ordinary patient."

* * *

"Please, go on," Dr. Sarîn Zavaryan says. "Go on, there's no need to rush; we have plenty of time." She presses the button on her recorder. Sertac Karan aka Dry-throated Sertac asks for a glass of water.

“Whenever the name of my ill-starred homeland *may-God-free-it* and all the ill-starred things we do to make it a *homeland* come to mind, like land and grave, like wind and rain, garden and orchard and dress and garb and house and home and farm and cane and water and river and fence and wall and stone and field and ridge and tree and bush and flower and grass and food and sound and song and subject and neighbor and worry and grief and land and sky and serf and man and tribe and everything else and so on and so forth, like succor and support, like rose and flower, village and city and crying and tears and science and art and women and children and the old and the elderly and odds and ends and laughing and crying and worries and woes and movement and bounty and family and kin and meadow and grass and name and fame and embroidery and pattern and boulder and rock and quarrel and tumult and roaring and rumbling and status and condition, like cold and freezing, like heart and head, brook and hill and night and day and fear and worry and lies and deceit and earth and hearth and house and home, like blood and flesh, like one and two, like mouth and tongue, like all those martyrs *may-they-rest-in-glory* who defended it against our *adversaries* who took it from us but couldn’t make it a home of their own, against the lust and ardor and passion and fantasy and insatiability of *those-who-make-this-life-unbearable*, no, I can’t remember when the name of that homeland began to be memorialized as *so-called*, when all of these places became *so-to-speak*s, when they turned into *probabilities*, when they descended to the level of *nothing*, when they became nothing but *sheer void*, I can’t remember when, finally, that homeland became an *unhappiness* and crashed into me. And because of that unhappiness, for a while now I can't go to any of the western provinces, I can't visit any of my friends, I can't wander as I wish, free of fear, along the streets and avenues and neighborhoods and squares of this city, I can't go down to the market, I can't be around people, I can't look into the shop windows, I can't get in a taxi and refuse to answer the driver's questions, my voice trembling, I can't walk the more I walk alone, I can't sit in a restaurant, I can't pass by the coffeehouses, I can't ask the shopkeepers for directions, I can't recline on the searing sands on the shore of some azure sea and lose myself in reverie as soon as I close my eyes—no, I can't do it anymore. For so long now I can't go anywhere, I can't go anywhere because of my *godforsaken-lifeless* color, because of my *godforsaken-bankrupt* identity, because of my *godforsaken-malignant* homeland, and it's enough already! Enough, enough, I am so fucking tired of this comedy, this lunacy, this depravity!"

"Yes," says Dr. Sarîn Zavaryan, "yes, I understand, but as I said, no need to rush, there are a number of words and expressions whose meanings I need to look up, but perhaps it's best for me to ask you directly. Please, go on, I'm listening."

"Yes," he replies. "Most of the time I don't understand either, you know. My father had this thing he always said, he probably heard it from his forefathers: *What is it that makes you so foul? God as my witness*, no matter how much I wash my hair with expensive shampoos, no matter how many colognes I spray on my chest and neck and armpits and crotch, no matter how much I shave my beard and thin my eyebrows, no matter how long I grow my hair, no matter how many different powders and foundations I use to mask my dark skin, no matter how many blonde-haired blue-eyed friends I make, I am always me, always the same Kurd, the same paragon of ignorance, the same bloodthirsty terrorist, the same *same* in their eyes. And I know myself well; no matter how much I change my face, my voice, my accent, my expressions, my perspectives, my dreams, I'll never be one of them. Like I said, I am *so-called* one of them, and no matter how much I work my ass off—excuse me—I'm stuck being *so-called* till hell freezes over."

"Till hell freezes over?"

"Yes, till hell freezes over," says Sertac Karan aka Gravedigger Sertac. "Please, don't record the rest of what I have to say, if by chance it's not necessary; let's continue without it."

"Why?" asks Dr. Sarîn Zavaryan.

"Why?"

Sertac Karan aka Taciturn Sertac wants to offer her a compelling answer in order to save himself from more of her questions, but he can't, he can't tell Dr. Sarîn Zavaryan of the twenty-two hellish days he spent in a torture chamber in this very city. He thinks immediately of the day he was taken from his home. They hadn't done anything to him at first, not even a slap on the wrist, but had simply asked questions like which school he worked at, what he studied and at which university, what his salary was, if he made more than them. But afterward, they brought him to a multistory building and locked him up in a dark cell before returning shortly thereafter and taking him to the torture chamber, hitting, kicking, insulting, and berating him the whole way, and then, without any apparent crime to speak of, they turned him like a screw so hard he lost his voice.

What had happened?

The police had caught one of those *motherfuckers* in his house with a few Picasso paintings—all fakes, obviously—and a few bottles of red mercury, and though there was no political angle there, when they made that *motherfucker* squeal without so much as raising a fist, things escalated from Picasso and the red mercury to his mom's pussy, and they didn't stop there. Sertac Karan aka You're-fucked Sertac didn't know the *motherfucker* or the other guys they arrested after him; but according to *Mercurial Picasso*'s statement—it eventually became a confession, causing his world to go black—he and Sertac Karan aka Washes-his-hands-of-politics Sertac had been part of the same faction, even though the faction had been disbanded after attacks from the traditionalists and after everyone else had gone home or fled to Europe, never to be seen again.

"Okay," the cop had said. "But what about that cassette? Whose voice is it, what the fuck is that song about?" And in a heartbeat the guy gave Sertac's name, Dengbêj Sertac, Sertac the Poet-Singer. "I don't know his last name, but it's Sertac's voice, he's, uh, he's singing about the liberation of the homeland. I'm begging you, brother, please don't let anything happen to my civil service job!"

* * *

Dr. Sarîn Zavaryan is waiting for an answer, provided that Sertac Karan aka Stuck-at-the-bottom-of-a-well Sertac can get himself out of there.

"It would be good if you turned that thing off," he says after a long silence. "I thought of something, a moment, from the past; that's why I stopped talking, I didn't know how to reply."

"Tell me about it, if you want," Dr. Sarîn Zavaryan says, taking the tape recorder off her desk and moving it to the corner of her office. Sertac Karan aka Scared-shitless Sertac watches her from the corner of his eye.

"You're hiding something," Dr. Sarîn Zavaryan says. "You've been keeping something from me since the beginning, something you won't tell me. What is it you're afraid of, Sertac? I'm not a cop, Sertac, you're not being interrogated, this isn't a torture chamber; whatever reports come out of here aren't going to the police station."

"I know," says Sertac Karan aka But-please Sertac with as much feeling as he can muster. "You don't have to tell me that. But please . . ."

"But please what? Look, I turned off the recorder and put it away, what else is there?"

"What else?" Sertac Karan aka Up-till-that-very-moment Sertac says to himself. "What else but total darkness?"

"Did you say something?"

"No, no, I didn't say anything."

"And you won't either."

"What I wanted to say was . . ."

"Yes?"

"Some of the things that happen in this city don't happen anywhere else in the world, that's what I wanted to say."

"Like what?"

"Like what?"

"Yes, like what?"

"Like sheer misery, for instance, and the poems written about sheer misery."

"I don't understand."

"Me neither," says Sertac Karan aka Hiding-himself Sertac in a whisper, losing himself in the depths of his besieged brain.

"I don't understand how you slip away so easily." Dr. Sarîn Zavaryan waves her hands at him. "Hellooooooooo, Earth to Sertac?"

Until that very moment, that moment when the Italian journalist apologized and took her purse off the stool beside the desk:

She had dug around for a while looking for a cassette.

No, first she had popped a full cassette out of her tape recorder.

She hurriedly scrawled *Sertac Karan, Volume: 01* on the J-card, and then that unpleasant, so-called patriotic bastard, burning with jealous curiosity, asked, "Is this the comrade you're interviewing?" with a tone of disgust in his voice.

After slipping the J-card back in the case, she gingerly inserted the cassette into its home.

Smiling sweetly again, she apologized to Sertac Karan aka Full-of-secrets Sertac.

She pressed the red *record* button for the second half of the interview; he was staring at the tape recorder the whole time. You'd think it wasn't the woman but the recorder that was interviewing him. Once upon a time—once upon a time!—he had wanted to get one of those small, fragile machines, to wander from village to village and catalogue words, sayings, folk songs, riddles, stories, tales, whatever folkloric thing he could find; but, for many different reasons—in fact, due to the series of events that turned the flow of his life in a completely impossible direction—this dream never came true; still, there was no sign of regret in him or in his words on the matter, but, sometimes a strange thing happens. He distracts the woman ever so briefly; he stops speaking in the middle of his sentence, purses his lips and lowers his head. He's on his way to another planet when she does what she thinks is best and intervenes, and at her "yes?" Sertac Karan aka Tragic-hero-Cembelî Sertac jolts like he's been woken from a gentle sleep or a scary dream and looks around himself with fearful eyes; looks at the woman, at her sullen interpreter, at the table and the things on it, and only then does he start speaking again.

Everything was going according to the woman's plan that day; the sun was out, shining gently, after the rain that had been falling since morning had stopped and the haze and smoke that had filled the square of the Upper Quarter had lifted. The army of aestheticized, or perhaps "whitewashed" was a better word, characters on the street—the children shining shoes or selling sunflower seeds, tissues, gum, and simit—had poured out of this godforsaken city's suffocating teahouses and its arcades, from under the eaves of its markets, *wormeaters* and *drunks* emerging from so many unknown sanctuaries, materializing out of nowhere onto the streets with their wretchedness, their misery, their poverty, their pitifulness on full display, wielding their stubborn clinginess as a browbeating strategy; with trays, boxes, and plastic bags in their hands, and with their messy hair, their eyelids dark green from sleeplessness or from bruises left by moms, dads, brothers, uncles, cousins, with their tattered clothes, their runny noses, their busted sandals and shoes, their feet without socks, their colorful dreams, they snuck into cafés, bakeries, and prep schools, timid, stammering, hungry and thirsty, wanting to talk, to do their best to hurriedly sell whatever they could. Speaking in broken Turkish, crippled bastards, hungry thugs, bootlicking soldiers, swindlers and vagabonds, burnouts, crooks, wrist cutters, stoners, junkies, and the rest of the streets' asswipes were brawling; as always, some compassionate souls took pity on them, felt bad for the children surrounded by roughnecks, sighing their not-very-sincere sighs, and before they bought the kids' tissues, their gum, a few fistfuls of sunflower seeds, those compassionate souls would rain down unsolicited advice on the kids, doing a full psychological evaluation of them before leaving them in the dust.

Who said those wretches were the children of the revolution? Who said they were the remnants of war? Sertac Karan aka Psychotic Sertac could see that those children were not more valuable than the red and shining rubble, rocks, and bricks paving the road to freedom; yes, that road wasn't their road, it wasn't suited to them, they had no road, the only road for them was the one they sealed off. He turned to the interpreter and with a burning heart said to her, "Leyla, please translate what I'm about to say word for word, because, well, how should I explain it? It's going to be a little confusing and indirect."

"A little confusing and indirect? You've been killing me all day! Not only are you subjecting me to everything you have to say, but then I've got to scrawl down my notes, gleaning what I can in an attempt to translate them as you trip over your tongue. You're completely oblivious to yourself, to me, and to that poor woman—good God, I hope your tongue falls out of your head! I was about to tell her we're through, the interview's over, but you, it's like you can read my mind, you want to keep jumping from thought to thought, even though nobody asked," she must have thought, but she smiled as she turned to Sertac Karan aka

Lower-Quarter Sertac and said, "Of course, brother Sertac, don't you trust my translation?"*

Sertac Karan aka Broken-mouthed Sertac paused for a second to dwell on this question, turned the word "trust" over and over in his head, compared it with a few other words, and spirited up some images to go with it, some memories.

But the issue wasn't just the war.

—*Long live Diyar!*

Nor its ruinous consequences.

—*Long live the brotherhood of the years!*

We were all children of that war.

—*Our pride and joy!*

"As if the war that occupies our conscious and subconscious twenty-four hours a day weren't enough, now the sociologists have descended upon us, for God's sake; they want to understand what happened to me, to us, in those years filled with nightmare after waking nightmare, even though I already knew I wasn't a *person*, well, no, I *was* a person, I *was* one of the most basic concepts in sociology, I was a bit of vocabulary, an entry in their lexicon, a broken, indecisive word, but those of us who took refuge in the cave were completely indecisive anyway. The cave would tell us things but we didn't believe it, we didn't believe in the fact that we were in a cave and that liberation was a distant fantasy. One day, one of us—a progressive-minded person—awoke in the night and proclaimed, 'The cave is lying, I saw it in my dream and in your dreams;

* Don't you trust my translation? (Trans.)

anyway, off to bed.' And before he fell back asleep, he asked, 'Whither freedom?' as we said to ourselves, "Off to bed!" and did the same."

"What cave?" asks Dr. Sarîn Zavaryan, and then she adds another entry in her observation report. The report is almost finished:

TO THE RELEVANT AUTHORITIES

This affidavit is to certify that the individual whose name and identifying information are listed above has attended his Psychotechnical Evaluation Assessment at the Psychotechnical Evaluation Center located at the address listed below, and that this Psychotechnical Evaluation Referral Report has been duly prepared by none other than myself, Dr. Sarîn Zavaryan. In the course of his psychiatric treatment, the aforementioned individual has demonstrated that he lost all grasp on reality long ago. Though forthcoming, he can go hours without speaking, without a single word coming out of his mouth, as though there is a fog in his brain. Persons who are in his life, or who were once in his life, both in the short and long term, have melded (and continue to meld) with characters in the stories he has written (and continues to write). In a similar manner, he has lost his ability to perceive the very notions of time and space. His cognitive functions are no longer adequate. While he does not believe in the existence of either a natural or supernatural power, sometimes he seeks refuge in God in ways that vary depending upon his emotional state, which fluctuates with different conditions, events, images, persons, and words; like the faithful, he will ask Him for help, and sometimes the individual in question even appears to behave like a Muslim devoted to the path of God. On one or two occasions, he even accompanied his father to the mosque.

He is disgusted by what Israeli soldiers do to Palestinian children; he cannot bear what is done to them; his eyes fill up with tears whenever it comes up. Similarly, he hates the racism of Arabs and the weakness Muslims show in the face of wealth, property, and women. According to him, such people will not go to Heaven.

Though he disavows any ideology, he admires Marxism and the notion of "classless society" that comes from it; because he accuses Turkish and Kurdish socialists, anarchists, feminists, and greens of insincerity and hypocrisy, he keeps his distance from them. Although he is not political, neither is he apolitical; in fact, he sustains himself on the dream of a righteous politics. Especially in times of violence, he is exceedingly sensitive to the issues, obstacles, and problems of the people. He says that the problem is not merely one of the society in which he lives, but that "the problem is the concept of society itself," by which means he abstracts himself from society. Additionally, though he is unhappy with his name, he does not want to take a new name.

His imagination is highly advanced. He writes stories but is not sure what he writes or what language he uses to do so.

The primary axis of his fantasies is erotic; more specifically, Decameronic.

He asserts that *Memories of My Melancholy Whores* is Márquez's greatest work.

As the course of his psychological treatment has proven, the aforementioned individual . . .

So spoke Sertac Karan aka Lost-in-reverie Sertac to himself, unable to find the courage to tell the imaginary character of Dr. Sarîn about events that had or had not happened. The other Sertac had won again; Sertac Karan aka Moments-ago Sertac had not left his house, had not even left his room, on that beautiful spring day that gave *normal* people the sense that the world is full of hope and life.

This story was his story, and it was possible it would go nowhere.

This story was his story, and it began fifteen years ago.

16

ONE HELLISH SUMMER day fifteen years ago, when the weather was so hot, it made you think twice about living—or at least it made the two people sitting next to him think twice about living—Sertac Karan aka Three-days-earlier Sertac was in a shared taxi full of people who didn't trust his ass, driving through one of the great gates that led into Amed—he can't remember which now, even despite the paranoid obsession with which he still thinks on, indeed cherishes, those long-lost days. Without any support, any weapon, any mustache, or any hope to his name, he realized that the Amed whose heart he was entering now was not the old Amed he had seen when he was eighteen years old. The first thing to confound him was the fact that the people in the city walked backward now; when he was eighteen, and he came and stayed with his uncle for twenty days so he could bring his mother to a good doctor in the city, the crowds all walked like him, which is to say like normal people, one foot after the other in their relentless onward march; nobody bumped into each other, at least as far as he saw, and even the city's drunks and junkies, even they kept to themselves as they tottered along.

What had happened to them? Why were they walking backward? Who had made them walk like that? Wasn't it cruel and unusual? Had they lost their minds? Or were they used to it? They had gotten used to it in the same way they had gotten used to so many other things, hadn't they?

Before the taxi driver dropped him off at Revolution Market —known now as Defeat Market—he made a proclamation that was almost a joke.

"*Heh heh heh* . . . Everything has changed, good buddy, everything has changed or has been changed; try not to look at the way people walk, man. *Heh heh heh.* Now get out and go walk among the people, listen to what they have to say. *Heh heh heh.* They even changed the city's name—now it's called NAH-med."

Until that very moment, Sertac Karan aka Until-that-very-moment Sertac had not believed it to be true, but after he took a few steps away from the vehicle, the taxi driver was proven correct: A tall, dark-skinned, thick-thighed girl appeared to his left; she was not alone but accompanied by a young bald guy in leather pants, and they held hands, walking, of course, backward toward the taxi stop. The guy was talking to her.

"Babe, I knocked back five bottles, you only had one, but just look at you, what a mess you are. *Ha ha ha.* Should we go to my place, or yours?"

"So what?" muttered Sertac Karan aka Just-for-the-hell-of-it Sertac to himself. "There's nothing surprising about it, the idiot's probably just making fun of me!"

The couple walked backward all the way until they got in the taxi, and Sertac Karan aka Wide-eyed Sertac couldn't take his eyes off the girl. She wore a pair of faded, tight, low-rise jeans, her stomach was visible, my God, in his whole life—could his be called a life?—he had never seen such a beautiful, such an attractive dark-skinned girl. In the Amed—now sadly known as NAH-med—of his youth, it wouldn't have been possible to see such a provocative outfit, let alone see a young girl walking around hand in hand with a bald guy, strolling around as they pleased. It was beyond imagination. From here it looked like the taxi driver opened the door with exaggerated courtesy, kneeling before them in a series of strange movements. Other than Sertac, nobody cast so much as a second glance at the girl and the pumpkin-headed guy in leather pants. Truly, nobody looked at them, least of all with bewilderment in their eyes. That day, he encountered dozens of young couples conversing comfortably as they strolled backward all over the city, somehow without bumping into anyone else, like they all had pairs of eyes in the back of their skulls as they gallivanted about with their horny smiles and their heads in the clouds. But beyond the strange outfits and the walking backward and the unflappability of the city's young people on that inauspicious day, he also saw other things. The city no longer had a beginning or an end; it sprawled. It had gotten so crowded; so many grand buildings were under construction; new roads had been built and the number of cars had multiplied, and consequently, of course, the amount of horn honking reached such heights, it could drive a man mad.

All the signs for the streets, avenues, and boulevards across the city had been taken down and replaced with signs in the three forbidden colors of the Kurdistan flag—green, yellow, red—and even the names had been altered, but the weirdest part was how the watermelon insignia, which was the symbol of the city, yes, that familiar insignia, was nowhere to be found, its place taken by a strange symbol he had never seen before in Amed, or anywhere in Kurdistan.

Sertac Karan aka That's-why Sertac was paying close attention, and couldn't decide whether he should laugh or cry.

Sertac Karan aka Emotional Sertac had come to this city one hellish summer day fifteen years ago in a shared taxi, and on the very same evening he had gone—walking normally—to stay with a friend in one of those totally wretched and derelict dormitories, a friend who wanted to liberate this city and all the cities in this Darkistan, and Sertac Karan aka All-alone-in-this-world Sertac stayed the night, and consequently a couple more nights, and before you knew it, he had been there for a month and a half—at his friend's request—without going outside even once. He didn't go out because he was afraid; his ID was old and tattered and his clothes weren't suited to the city. He wore white tennis shoes, brown cotton pants, and a gray button-down shirt, and he did not look at all like he belonged in this city. So many people came and went from this house; a girl who was short and couldn't really be considered pretty would come and sit in the other room and pluck away poorly on a tembûr that was longer than her body into the wee hours of the morning, while other people would come at all hours and sit and smoke and drink tea for hours on end as they discussed the liberation of the homeland and the best tactics for achieving liberation; most of the time, Sertac Karan aka Ass-backward

Sertac would chime in with his two cents, though in the end nobody ever managed to persuade anybody else of anything.

The cat in the house hated him; that Most Blessed of God's creatures had been circling him since his arrival, waiting for her chance to pounce. You would think Sertac Karan aka Pussycat Sertac had murdered the cat's dad or something, because she would raise her hackles angrily whenever she saw him.

One of his friends chided him gravely. "Don't mess with the cat, brother Sertac. Try not to make eye contact, and do your best to hide yourself. She has some kind of psychological disorder—she can't stand the word 'revolution.'"

It beggared belief: For the first time in his life, Sertac Karan aka Getting-by Sertac was hearing it was possible for a Lake Wan cat to lose her shit over the word 'revolution'; the state of things between them nonetheless grew only worse. It's not like Sertac did anything to the cat; the cat was just fucking with him. One day, when the cat went to the living room to watch some TV show about butchers, he hid behind the kitchen door and shouted in order to gauge the cat's reaction.

"Revolution, revolution, revolution!"

The cat turned in an instant, and before she could bare her claws to pounce on him with a truly bone-chilling meow, Sertac slammed the door and didn't emerge from the kitchen until nightfall. It was now clear to him: Both people and cats had changed their temperaments, and both had turned on revolution, which was now orphaned and all alone in this world.

* * *

Sertac Karan aka Process Sertac was so incredibly bored and had no idea what he was doing there, what he was saying, or whom he was saying it to. He would drag himself unwillingly from the bed every morning, wearing a sourpuss expression—because he didn't want to wash his face—and a wifebeater and shorts, and he would sit and enjoy himself in front of the TV in the musty living room, and after rolling a few cigarettes he would go out onto the balcony where his friends slept and wake them each, one by one, in order to make breakfast according to a menu that never changed: cheese and melon and NAH-med bread and tea.

This was his job: making these wake-up calls. After so many years in exile, so many years of labor and toil and hustle and bustle and sleepless and dreamless nights, now, Sertac was here, in a city laughing about how far it had fallen, in a house whose four walls were guarded by a cat that had lost its mind, in a windowless room containing nothing more than a busted mattress. He was bored, no, he was fucked; he only felt any semblance of relief when he read a book, but the arrival of the short, ugly girl always took that pleasure from him too. In theory, she came to this house to learn what it means to be a revolutionary, but, in practice, she was there to surround herself with young men, each more handsome than the last. One day in particular, before she began torturing both the tembûr and his friends' ears, she started prattling on about feminism, bookending her lecture with a statement almost tailor-made to irk Sertac.

"You know, Rosa Luxemburg may have been short, but she still made history."

Up until now, Sertac Karan aka Attentive-listener Sertac had not chimed in, but when she brought up Rosa, he rejoined her critique with a critique of his own.

"There's something you're forgetting, though, sister, which is that Rosa didn't play the tembûr and she wasn't prowling for a man."*

And this *sister* was petrified, frozen in place like someone had just poured boiling water over her, like her brain had gone out of order, her mouth agape as she stared at Sertac. And her long, long look at him was the last look she ever gave anyone in that house, because, with her ego bruised, she took hold of the neck of her tembûr and got herself out of there. All of Sertac's friends thanked him; some even asked to kiss his hand.

"Bless that mouth of yours, Sertac—you saved us from that nightmare!"

She left. All it had taken was a few choice words and she had left, taken her tembûr and left them alone, and yet with her departure a still greater nightmare showed its face, for how could they have known "Sertaco" was not their old Sertac? How could they have known what had been hiding under the surface of that calm, quiescent sea? It was Sertac's turn now. Whatever symptoms there were for madness, he displayed every last one of them to his friends over the course of an incredibly sleepless twenty-four hours, leading to the formation of two camps within the house, disputing whether or not he really had gone mad.

Some of them insisted, "He's teasing us; he's making a show of madness, and as you can see, he plays the part well."

* Plus, they executed her. (Trans.)

While the others argued, "If he didn't lose his mind, then why did he get completely naked and tie his arms and legs with IV tubing? If he's not crazy, then why did he tear up a copy of *Das Kapital* and eat every last page?"

They argued and argued, each accusing the other side of ignorance, of stupidity, and after the IV tubing and the paper eating, Sertac put on another display of madness: He picked up a knife, carved a swastika into a watermelon, and called his friends to come eat a snack. Nobody got close to him with the knife still in his hand, and when he realized they weren't going to eat, he cried out angrily.

"Tell me, what singer represented Turkey with what song at the 1983 Eurovision Song Competition? Quick! One, two, three."

But alas! Who would know something like that?

A few of them said, "Let's keep him talking. He's off his rocker. We'll take him down."

The others retorted, "No, no, we can't do it like that, it'd be a shame. We mustn't hurt him, let's wait him out; he can babble on till morning as long as he puts down the knife."

Sertac Karan aka Illegal Sertac kept counting. "Six, seven, eight, nine . . . and teeennnnnn, and teeennnnnn, God's put His hand up my ass again!"

Shocked, his friends scurried awkwardly to the corners of the room. They would never have expected anything like this from Sertac. They hadn't accounted for the possibility that a wise, militant, well-read, and well-traveled revolutionary with so many years of experience could so quickly lose his marbles. All told, he hadn't left the house for a month and a half, hadn't gone anywhere except the balcony; he'd imprisoned himself inside because his ID was old and because he didn't know the new order of things in the city; he hadn't eaten anything but cheese, watermelon, and NAH-med bread; he hadn't asked after things in the Upper Committee; worst of all, even though his family had settled in the same city, he hadn't gotten the chance to visit them, on the grounds that it wasn't "secure"—their word, not his. No, nobody believed such a tenderhearted and coolheaded and steadfast person could make such a demand of the Upper, and, at any rate, who had the balls to bring such small, worthless, paltry, and absurd concerns and demands to the Upper? Was it up to them? Was the Upper of today the same as their fathers' Upper? Thank God he hadn't attempted anything like that, thank God the wishes of a stark-raving madman hadn't been communicated to the Upper, and thank God they managed to take care of the situation themselves. Everything—yes, everything, down to dreams, down to involuntary reflexes like laughing out of turn or crying or blinking or yawning—needed to be precisely as it appeared on his records, down to the very last comma.

That morning, Sertac Karan aka Bird-in-the-hand Sertac wore himself out with frenzy and sleeplessness, and when he could stand no longer, his friends came out of their corners, surrounded him, took the knife out of his hands, and held his arms tight as they carried him to his room, laid him out in bed, and gave him a powerful sedative so he wouldn't remember what had happened once he woke up. That night, Sertac Karan aka Sedated Sertac had a dream only semiotic oneirologists—absolutely nobody else—would be able to interpret: He was in

Amed; he had, in fact, come to Amed from somewhere far away, but he was here now, in this city of cities, this king among cities, the city of his childhood dreams, the city of his long-suffering and quite beloved Kurds. He couldn't remember much of the dream, just a few snippets, but nonetheless, the next day he recounted what he could remember to his friends.

"It was a dream full of weird stuff. I was in the city's biggest, most crowded market, but I didn't know where I was going. The police were swarming everywhere, and I mean *everywhere*, from the bus stops and the shops and stores to the kiosks and cafés and barbers and hairdressers; the whole market was being combed, top to bottom. They were checking IDs, and anyone whose ID was old and tattered was arrested on the spot. The paddy wagon was stuffed to the brim with people, and a select handful of cops, whose cheeks and noses and helmets and shields were painted with our beloved shades of green and yellow and red, used their colorful truncheons to randomly beat the screaming and shouting people inside. I was afraid; I was so afraid, my whole body was trembling. I had already taken out my wallet before they even called me over and asked for my ID. I walked toward a group of cops so they wouldn't be suspicious of me. Yes, that was my goal. I pitied myself as I walked toward them, and I prayed to God that He would send me a miracle and save me from the hands of those villains, but I didn't really expect much from the Lord Of All Worlds because I am a Nonbeliever and I quit reading the Qur'an when I was still very young, and as a child I would make fun of the call to prayer, and whenever my dad rolled out his prayer mat to pray, I would stand in front of him and sing "The Internationale." All of these things flashed before my eyes like a strip of film, and so I gave up hoping in God, but He did not give up on me. He took mercy on me and sent a witch to my aid, because when I was about to hand over my ID to the police—exactly at the right moment—she descended in a halo glowing with the three forbidden colors and saved me from being beaten, from being arrested, from being subject to an unknown fate. We flew away from there, or rather, she flew away; I rode on her back, and we went somewhere I didn't know. We were airborne, and I asked her where we were going, but she didn't give two shits about my question, or maybe she was hard of hearing. Anyway, we went on like that for a while, and then, yes, she descended smoothly and with aplomb, like a plane landing, and she landed in an empty field, or else I didn't see anything else around us. As soon as her feet touched the ground, she flung me off her back and I hit the ground hard. I didn't understand why she'd done something so antagonistic after saving me. I started to feel afraid again. This must be the Devil herself, I thought to myself, and she laughed as if she could hear my thoughts, and that's when I noticed her teeth. I froze up because her teeth were long and sharp and bloody. I stumbled backward involuntarily, trying to get away from her, but she only surprised me even more by lifting up her skirts to show me what she had down there. And down there it was, how should I say, like a mouth with teeth all its own, and my own teeth, which I hadn't brushed in a long time, began chattering, because I was overcome with fear and she wanted to catch me. She asked me the first question, and a weird dialogue between us developed from there.

"'Do you know who I am?'

"'Nah-nah-no.'

"'I am Pîra NAH, Witch of the NO.'

"'Witch of the what?'

"'NO.'

"'Witch of the NO?'

"'Yes, Witch of the NO. Don't you recognize my mouth or my teeth?'

"'I do, but I couldn't bring myself to say it, I don't have the . . .'

"'You don't have the courage . . . Do you know how old I am?'

"'No, but I can guess.'

"'You can guess? Well then . . . Did you see my pussy?'"

Sertac was silent.

"'I said, did you see my pussy?'

"'I didn't go looking for it, but you did show it to me, though, yes, with its lips and teeth. What kind of pussy is that?'

"'Are you afraid?'

"'Well, I've never seen anything like it.'

"'Never seen what? Pussy? Or pussy with teeth?'

"'You are one nasty hag!'

"'I am your grandma.'

"'Enough already!'

"'I am your mama.'

"'Get out of here, you disgusting bitch!'

"'I am your aunt.'

"'Your filthy mouth. Please stop, for the love of God!'

"'I am your ruined country.'

"'You're my dick! You hear me?'

"'Stick your dick in your mama, in your sister, you mongrel!'

"'Why are you cursing at me like this? Have you no shame?'

"'But it was you. You started it!'

"'My God, why have you forsaken me? I wanted to be saved from the police, and now . . .'

"'What do you mean "and now"? Women scare the shit out of you.'

"'Fuck off!'

"'Pussy makes you lose your mind.'

"'Shame, shame on you—shame on your white hair and your wrinkled face!'

"'I am your shame.'

"'You're nothing to me!'

"'I'm a friend to *Pîra Torê*.'

"'You're not even a slipper at Pîra Torê's door!'

"'I am your defeated struggle.'

"'Our struggle, our revolution has not been defeated! We've just postponed it, is all.'

"'To postpone is to give in to defeat.'

"'What are you, the witch philosopher? Fuck you a hundred times over!'

"'Women scare the shit out of you.'

"'Women like you scare the shit out of me.'

"'I am your conceited literature, the sum of every word every Kurd has ever written.'

"'Enough already!'

"'Fate, I am your fate.'

"And as soon as she said, 'I am your fate,' she pulled out a dagger from between her tits and plunged it into the left side of her chest, so it would go through her heart. I froze where I stood as she began giggling again, but not a single drop of blood came out of her, and then her wrinkled face began changing ever so slowly; the lines and folds vanished little by little, and the witch turned into a beautiful woman. I stepped closer and inspected this magical transformation. I wanted to touch her down there, because it was becoming normal and it looked so beautiful; it was shining, those plump lower lips dewy and colorful and blooming like spring flowers, and then, and then a harsh light—a light so strong, it was blinding—shot out from there and hit me in the face, and before I could get to her, she took to the air and flew, flew, flew until she vanished from sight, flew until I was there all alone. And that's right when I woke up. I woke up to the sound of music. And that was my dream."

Once Sertac Karan aka Withheld Sertac finished telling his friends about his dream, they exchanged looks of bewilderment with one another. They had no idea what to say, and so they said nothing at all. From that day forth, nobody messed with him. The decision had been made by the Upper: For some time, nobody was to approach him, nobody was to assign him any work, and he was to be left to his own devices. Rumor had it that they planned to send an inspector to conduct an investigation into the matter.

* * *

Sertac Karan aka Addled Sertac had come to this city one hellish summer day fifteen years ago; he had come to this city whose names and pronouns and shapes and forms and culture had changed entirely, and where people walked backward and the word *revolution* had suddenly been made *yasax*,* and where the symbol of this once-great city, the watermelon, had been stripped away and replaced with a swastika, and slowly but surely Sertac Karan aka Revo-revolution Sertac came to understand what had happened both to him and to the revolution.

* Where the Turkish word "yasak," meaning "banned" or "prohibited," ends in a hard, definitive "k" sound, this moment of code-switching here ends with the Kurdish letter "x," a letter pronounced in the back of the throat, closest to the phoneme "kh," which is to say, a consonant less definitive, more open-ended, more ambiguous, and do not all prohibitions have their fugitivities? Is there not always an escape route, a way out, from the most draconian bans? Even the letter "x" demolishes the upright bar of the "k" for something more wayward, and is that not in and of itself a revolution? (Trans.)

PART THREE
Signifier

17

THAT EVENING, THE Director of the Foundation for Defeated Writers, Frau Lili Müller, collected Sertac and his two overstuffed suitcases from Düsseldorf Airport and drove him to the Münster city center, and from there to the *Diakonissenmutterhaus* guesthouse, where he would be staying; before she left him, she handed him an envelope containing exactly six thousand euros, his stipend, and asked him to count it out, to make sure there had been no mistake with the math. But, not wanting to count those crisp new euro bills one by one in front of her, he used his broken English to thank Frau Müller for everything. Once Frau Müller left, he locked the door and made that stack of bills rain on his bed and then flung himself on top.

At first, he couldn't believe he was there, in Münster, in a tiny room in this enormous guesthouse. Then, after a very long shower and a leisurely cigarette—intentionally disregarding the sign in the room prohibiting smoking—then and only then did he begin coming to his senses and inspecting the order of things in the room.

His bed was underneath a window that stretched across the whole wall, and on his Gothic-style bedside table—his request—there was a Bible, which had to be gotten rid of as soon as possible. Per his wishes, they also put an antique desk and chair next to the bed, because he was going to write without stopping; and the desk lamp—his request as well—had not been forgotten either. He put his as-yet-unwritten-in notebook, along with a couple of fountain pens and a couple of thematically similar books, on the table. He brought very few books with him, to reduce his load: Goethe, Yeats, Handke, and Arab Shamilov.

The shower and the toilet were side by side. The biggest problem he would have was with the enormous *a la franca* toilet. The solution was easy: Every time he took a shit, he would get in the tub and wash himself off; otherwise there was no hope of staying clean.

Before going to sleep, he lined up his hygiene and cosmetic products—two shampoos, a box of Q-tips, toothpaste, two brushes, a bottle of aftershave, a deodorant, a light cologne, nail clippers, tweezers, a few creams, and some ointments—on the bathroom shelf. The wardrobe was opposite the bathroom, and in three of its narrow cubbies he stored his finer clothes, which had been washed in Amed water, while the rest he stuffed with socks, T-shirts, linen pants, two sets of underwear, two sets of undershirts, and three pairs of light summer shoes. He took out two pairs of slippers: one for the bathroom and one for the bedroom.

Sertac had been in Amed that very morning. At the café in the airport, he chain-smoked anxiously as he drank his expensive tea. The place was full of Kurds who spoke Soranî, coming from South Kurdistan to go to Stenbol, and from there to who knows what European country. Some of them were perhaps headed for America or Canada. The jittery excitement of his trip caught up with him in the café, so full of cigarette smoke, he felt like he was suffocating. At the same time the gloom, the sorrow of separation, the grief of leaving a woman and, especially, a city behind all weighed heavy on his heart, and there, right there, next to a sweet little girl asking curious questions in her sweet little Soranî to her indifferent father, he wanted to cry his eyes out.

He had been at Dr. Sarîn's house that very morning. He woke up at the crack of dawn with the trilling of the alarm clock and went to the bathroom. He shaved his two-day-old beard and showered. Then, he took one last look at the suitcases sitting, mouths agape, in the room he never left, as if to ask them if anything was missing, but there was nothing missing.

* * *

He had been in Amed that very morning, at Dr. Sarîn's house, watching over her, her head wrapped in a scarf to relieve a headache. She was sleeping, and in her sleep she looked even more innocent. He couldn't bring himself to wake her up, to say, "I'm headed out," so he wrote a note on a Post-it and stuck it to the big mirror before leaving. He looked at her face for a while, at her closed eyes, at her lips, which would no longer touch his lips, and then his eyes landed on her crotch, which had been invaded a few days earlier when, before coming to term, a bit of him and a bit of her had been removed and tossed into some trash can brimming with blood.

He had been in Amed that very morning, in the always-and-ever abortive city of Amed, and his liver spilled its black blood all over the floor of the airport. Dirty children appeared in his path, asking for money. He pointed at the trail of his black blood.

* * *

Apart from him, the nun with the limp who had been whining about him since the moment of his arrival, and the female student who knew nothing about him except that he was living there, there was nobody else staying in the guesthouse. On his first day there, he descended the wide, tall stairway to have breakfast and to do a little bit of exploring, and he found himself in a spacious but empty dining room.

Breakfast was on the house, but he would have to pay for all his other meals. A middle-aged woman with a cheerful face welcomed him with a heartfelt *guten morgen*, to which he replied in English, and for some time thereafter they stared at each other blankly without speaking. The woman only served the guests tea and coffee; they had to serve themselves the rest. On a table festooned with colorful flowers were all the staples of a traditional German breakfast: salami and sausages made of pork, scrambled eggs with bacon made of pork, various cheeses (chiefly *butterkäse*[*]), crunchy granola, big green and black olives, various yogurts, honey and jam, little packets of butter, fruit and fruit juices, milk and cream, pâté, potatoes, and every last type of German bread.

He couldn't decide where to begin, so just stood there in front of the table admiring its bounty, until eventually he decided on orange juice and knocked back a couple of glasses of it as he stood there; eventually he piled his plate high to let himself have a taste of everything, and as if that weren't enough, he went back for seconds, this time charging at the German breads like he was stricken by famine. Breakfast finished at ten o'clock, and he had come downstairs at seven.

Frau Müller and her assistant, Ozlem, who would be working as his interpreter on the project, were going to collect him from the guesthouse at eleven o'clock. After a brief tour of the city center, according to the plan, lunch would be at an Italian restaurant, where Frau Müller was going to introduce him to three other writers who had arrived in Münster the week before. This was the whole point of the project; the four writers were to use the meal as an excuse to sit together and discuss the writing they intended to do in Münster.

* Invented in 1927, and one of the fattier cheeses there are, butterkäse is an underappreciated testament to the Weimar Republic's creative ingenuity. According to *Fundamentals of Cheese Science*, butterkäse is a soft, surface-ripened, brine-salted cheese that has holes (known scientifically as "eyes"). "What happens to the hole," asks Bertolt Brecht, "when the cheese is gone?" What happens to the eye, or the I, for that matter, when the cheese is gone? (Trans.)

Five minutes before eleven, Sertac Karan aka Promise-made-promise-kept Sertac stood outside the front door of the guesthouse, holding the leather briefcase Dr. Sarîn had given him as a gift; it contained a couple of books in Kurdish. Waiting for his ride, he checked out the houris who passed by from time to time, the houris who looked like identical twins, pale-white bodies that had never seen real sunlight, the blondest and most golden women of the Aryan race, along with their men, a hundred times more privileged and more entitled than the women were, and their immaculate, prissy dogs and their almost-weightless bicycles, some running, some strolling, some cycling, some walking their dogs without leashes and without fear of consequences, all making their way to or from the largest promenade in the whole city, which was near the guesthouse. He was surrounded by trees and colorful flowers, by the sounds of birds and frogs in harmony with the bells and the piano someone was playing nearby, producing the most unparalleled symphony he had ever heard. A few elderly people sat on benches in the yard, which was enlivened by cherry trees, in the pale light of the sun, talking to one another of some bygone ideology that had once ground millions of people to dust. Sertac Karan aka Ready-and-willing Sertac was there, standing in wait at the door to the guesthouse, which had no beginning and no end. Frau Müller and Ozlem arrived right on time, and after a brief exchange of pleasantries they set out for the city center.

On the way, Ozlem asked Sertac Karan aka Flabbergasted Sertac if he could ride a bicycle, and Sertac Karan aka Pedal-to-the-metal Sertac smiled and replied, "Never mind a bicycle, I can't even ride a tricycle."

* * *

They were at the largest market in the city, and Sertac Karan aka Wide-eyed Sertac listened to Ozlem as he admired the rather expensive clothes in the boutique windows. Ozlem was translating, word for word, every last thing Frau Müller said into Turkish, occasionally interjecting additional comments of her own: "Don't listen to her, brother Sertac, Münster is such a bleak place"; "It's famous for its solitude"; "Maybe it'll make you lose a gasket in no time, that is, if you can even find a gasket in the first place." And she smiled beautifully as her eyes lingered on him. The market, with paths and walkways made of square, shining tiles of varying designs, received tourists into its open arms, their frenzied tempo lasting into the evening when, according to Ozlem, they would continue on their way to the cafés, bars, and restaurants, where they would linger late into the night.

A malaise welled up in him, brought on by this misbegotten stroll, because Sertac Karan aka Diffident Sertac didn't give a shit about the fountain in the square or the city's churches and monasteries or the philandering tourists; he only wanted to go to the promenade, which he could partially see from his room, and the name of which had come up a few times as they left the guesthouse. He had seen topless girls on the lawns, just lying around, splayed out, resting and relaxing, untroubled, unbothered, not a care in the world, with their human rights, with freedom, with the uncanniness of the word "freedom," with the concept of democracy, not needing to pay a second thought to any of the death or the killing, to the bombs that go off out of nowhere, to the prisons and to the torture chambers, to raids and arrests, to the sheer inhumanity of it all, just lying around, splayed out, resting and relaxing. Arriving at the restaurant, those images and thoughts continued to plague him, kept the ache thumping in his head.

The other guests had already begun drinking and were chatting warmly. Frau Müller introduced him to the other three before they sat down; there was the Afghan, Taher Parvan, seated next to the Iraqi, Sadiq el Behri, across from the Dane, May Bing, and a few other people from the institute.

Taher was a poet, about the same age as Sertac; a tall, dark-skinned, gaunt man. Wearing black pants with a drop crotch, a green shirt with pockets and so many buttons—the same shirt in the photo of him that appeared in the authors' catalogue—and a pair of white tennis shoes, which he must've bought here in Münster, he called to mind not so much a poet as a "Defeated" monkey, smiling a very toothy smile with teeth yellowed by tobacco and hashish as he took hold of Sertac's hand and shook it and shook it and shook it. Sertac replied to Taher with the same warmth, politely enjoining him to please, sit back down.

Sadiq el Behri was short and bald, had a thin mustache, and, according to the information in the brochure, had been born four years prior to Sertac Karan aka Fuck-your-mother Sertac, and he had published four collections of short stories. He was bedecked in a shimmery gray three-piece suit and a starched white shirt, with all due respect for the significance of the occasion. He didn't act like their Afghan colleague; when Sertac Karan aka Shy Sertac extended his hand for a handshake, the Iraqi took it languidly in his fingertips without getting up and nodded his head half-heartedly in greeting at Sertac, seemingly self-satisfied, the dour expression on his face almost asking, "And what have we here?" The unpleasantry of it all made the guests all look at one another, perplexed and awkward, until Frau Müller intervened quickly to turn him to May, whose turn it was for him to meet. Sertac Karan aka Va-va-voom Sertac realized, as soon as he turned to May, why Sadiq was sulking, because before him was not just a beautiful Danish woman, but a nymph. May was completely different than the black-and-white photograph of her in the brochure; her hair was not that hair, her visage was not that visage, her eyes were not those eyes, and her lips were not those lips. With her pure-white breasts swaddled in a low-cut green dress, May greeted him by bowing her head as though she were appearing before an emperor, with so much gravitas that everyone laughed. Before he sat down, she told him she liked the brief piece of writing he had included in the catalogue.

Sertac Karan aka Hung-up-on-May Sertac sat beside May and hung his bag on the chair. He put two packs of cigarettes—one of them half finished—and a cheap lighter on the table and glanced at Sadiq to see how he was faring.

They remained at the Italian restaurant well past lunch, drinking and eating late into the night while the Germans footed the bill. One bottle would end and another would arrive, and Sertac Karan aka Storyteller Sertac would raise his glass occasionally to Sadiq's, in a conciliatory gesture, and would cheers in Kurdish: "*Noşşş!*"

* * *

Sertac Karan aka Browbeater Sertac never saw Sadiq el Behri again after that night, neither in Münster nor in any other part of Germany. Rumor had it he went to Frau Müller the following day and requested that she send him to Bochum, to join the other writers there. Without giving it much thought, she sent off Sadiq in her own car. Sertac Karan aka Making-amends Sertac lost no time in sending Sadiq a few apology emails, but he got no response. Here is what Sertac Karan aka Up-to-a-certain-point Sertac wrote in one such email:

Dear Sadiq,

My Good Brother,

First of all, I want to apologize for my inappropriate and meaningless actions and rude behavior that unfortunate night. My guilt and my shame stretch from here to Bochum, and you are in the right from there to the door of my bedroom. You don't have to reply, but I wanted to write to tell you what's on my mind. To tell you the truth, I don't remember what happened in the restaurant. I do know the wineglass I threw at you hit you on the head. I swear to God, in my entire life I have never brawled with anyone, never beat up anyone, never had any hostility toward anyone. I'm very sensitive, and more than that, I am a humanist, and so I don't—I can't!—be mean to anyone. But all the world's trials and tribulations came and found me nonetheless. No matter what I do, I have a penchant for trouble. As a result, I always either get my head broken or, at the very least, a few of my ribs.

But coming back to that night: Yes, what happened that night? Everything was normal; we ate and drank, we laughed, we bantered, we joked, we read poems, we told each other about our misadventures and about the situations back in each of our countries, but really it was just me and Taher. You were totally silent; from time to time, you would direct questions to Ozlem and Frau Müller, and I turned my ear to everything they said. Yes, brother, I remember very clearly when you asked her directly, "Tell me, Frau Müller, where did you find this feudal Kurd?" Yes, Sadiq, dear, dear Sadiq, that was verbatim what you said to that kind woman, no more and no less. Hell, man, do I have feudalism written on my forehead? What on Earth made you call me feudal? Sure, I might not speak English as well as you, but then again, my parents were never fucked so hard by British soldiers that they learned English. No, it was always you who fucked us... But it's just not possible for it to be a coincidence that the words "feudal" and "Kurd" ended up next to each other in a sentence, now, Sadiq, it's simply not possible! I'm not someone who likes to use nasty words; I don't want to swear, I really don't, but my fucking God, Sadiq, what did you mean by feudal? Please, tell me, what does feudal mean to you? After I came and smashed a glass on your head, you—how shall I put it politely?—lost your shit, you bad-mouthed the great Arab Shamilov, which really cut me to the bone, truly broke my heart, and so after the glass I had no choice but to slam the bottle against the side of your head. It was the first time in my life I ever had to deal with the German police, in their green uniforms, but God bless you, you chose not to press charges, and everything was resolved right then and there.

In sum, it's good that you went. You did the right thing by chugging your wine and leaving Münster before you got the chance to have sex with May. Please rest assured that as I write this email, literally this very moment, May is with Taher, yes, yes indeed, she is with Taher the Afghan, and who on God's green Earth knows what kinds of naughty things they're doing to each other! As for me, I talk a big game. I'm thunder without rain, as they say, but I don't have any tricks up my sleeve; I'm all talk, no game, maybe a kiss or two...

Question 1: Sadiq, you are of Kurdish descent, aren't you?

Question 2: Why did you lose your mind and lash out at me?

If you only did it for Danish May, then I pray God delivers your due punishment. But if you did it just because I'm also a Kurd, then I pray you won't live to see another day!

Take care of yourself, man . . .

Your Kurdish brother Sertac Karan

* * *

This story was his story, and it was in Kurdish.

This story was his story, and it was slipping out of his control.

In the meantime, Sertac Karan aka Feudal Sertac was in search of a feudal guy with big balls.

In the meantime, Sertac Karan aka Oppressed Sertac longed for a colonized city, and dwelt on the reveries and the dreams he had for it.

18

IT WAS RARE for Sertac Karan aka Obsessive Sertac to go any farther than the places he knew best—the four blocks around the guesthouse, a few streets nearby, and the city center—even if he carried with him the city map he'd bought for eight euros. He spread out the map, six sheets of A4 paper, on the table and used a red marker to circle the guesthouse and a few other places, and since he would be using it so often, he taped it all over with grave solemnity, especially the parts where it folded, so it wouldn't tear too soon, and whenever he woke up, even on the days he wasn't going out, the map waited open on the table for him, inviting him to continue marking it up.

A few days earlier, he'd chanced upon a bar while on a walk; it had taken him less than ten minutes walking at his normal pace to get to the street it was on. He entered in the afternoon and drank until the middle of the night, and as the hours passed a number of blonde-haired, blue-eyed girls arrived, brightening up the dark and desolation of the tiny bar, their revelry ensconcing itself in his stomach first by a giant beer and then by tequila.

He prepared to do the same thing again tonight. He changed into a long-sleeved black T-shirt and a pair of black pants and left the guesthouse, which he had renamed Boredom Central, bringing with him two hundred euros and, of course, his map, his passport, and the book by Arab Shamilov. He crossed the wide, chaotic promenade and ran into a few high-school students. Still wearing their uniforms, they were celebrating something with flowers and champagne. One of them called out after him. "Heyyyy! Heyyyy!" It was a girl, brandishing a half-empty champagne bottle at him and inviting him to join them. Sertac Karan aka Congenial-and-approachable Sertac smiled at her, and replied in a way that surprised even himself, with a sentence he thought he had accurately memorized from the *Guide to Learning English* he had brought with him to Münster. "Thank you anyway, but I am already on way to bar." He didn't want to join a conversation with those dangerous high schoolers, and at any rate, when she realized he wouldn't be joining them, the girl swore and insulted him in two languages, then flashed her pale-white tits at him, and the boys, all laughing, bared their asses at Sertac Karan aka Ever-doomed Sertac. Sertac Karan aka Storyteller Sertac consoled himself by saying, "How could you have known?" Really, how could they have known this scene would end up in his story after he got home? They didn't know, nobody knew, neither they nor the people at the bar where he would soon be arriving.

* * *

Sertac Karan aka A-good-egg Sertac asked the bartender—a tall, sturdy girl was serving tonight—for a pint of dark beer, and he took Arab Shamilov's novel *Şivanê Kurmanca* aka The Kurdish Shepherd out of his bag and laid it out on the bar with tremendous care, like he was handling a Qur'an, and he laughed as he said to himself, "A stout beer and *Şivanê Kurmanca*." The beer came quickly, but before he took his first sip, he lit a cigarette and turned his ear to the sweet, pleasant music. The girl had tried to change the music upon his arrival, but he stopped her. "Let this play," he said, "I love jazz," before turning his focus to a page in the novel. It wasn't really all that cool out, but the occasional breeze would blow in suddenly as the rain began sprinkling down.

Apart from an old man, there were no other customers at this hour. After she finished her tasks, the bartender came with a cocktail, sat down beside Sertac Karan aka Completely-unexpected Sertac, and asked what he was reading. He attempted, as best he could in his limited English, to say something about Arab Shamilov, talking about, for instance, his long illness. She wasn't from here; she had come from Ukraine, from the city of Volodymyr, to the city of Köln. She spent two years in Köln; she spoke English, and in no time at all got German under her belt too. She worked various jobs to get by during her years in Köln. Now she was enrolled at the Münster *Kunstakademie*, where she was studying classical art history, but she had given up hope of ever graduating. In her opinion, Münster was the very epitome of horror and anguish. As if to prove her point, she brought up the movie *The Truman Show* as an example. Yes, Sertac Karan aka Utterly-breathless Sertac had seen it, and not just once or twice.

Münster was the world's largest insane asylum; so why had he chosen Münster? Why not Berlin? Sertac Karan aka Please-go-on Sertac explained from beginning to end the ordeal of his choosing a city. Münster hadn't been his preference, he hadn't requested it, but the people who extended him the invitation to Münster had nonetheless done so with good intentions. He was from Amed, had she ever heard of Amed? Oh-ho-ho! He was from a city of unending chaos and clamor, a tough, gritty, difficult, hostile city full of violence. From a city of washed corpses and corpse washers, from a city of arrogance, from a city where the most vicious brutality takes place, which is why the Germans sent him straight to Münster, to wrap his wounds, to heal his spirit, to revitalize him completely, but they hadn't considered that the more he asked of Münster, the more it responded in kind with its lethal malaise. The girl wasn't wrong, after all; Münster really was a lethal place for someone like him, a place for an anonymous death, a place for dying entirely lonely and entirely alone, because apart from the croaking of the frogs and the cheeping of the birds and the tolling of the bells and the sudden claps of thunder, there was no other sound of life. Had they plugged his ears with wax? Had he gone deaf? Why couldn't he hear? Sertac Karan aka Pleasant-conversation Sertac had embarked on an insane soliloquy and forgotten about the girl altogether. Yes, he had come from Amed, where there were a few words only ever spoken there, a few political phrases that meant absolutely nothing anywhere else except Amed. Was it possible to be arrested in Münster and to rot in prison for no reason at all? What motherfucker was wasting away in there right now, and on what grounds? What was the mayor of Münster doing right this second? Did Münster have that kind of collective known as "crowds"? Who sacrificed themselves here, and for what? Why is our blood so cheap? Which was when the girl took her leave, needing to tend to another customer. Perhaps she was unsettled by his silence, but had he really been silent? His glass was empty, and he had to piss something bad.

The bar slowly filled with all kinds of customers, and the bartender's workload only grew and grew; she ran from one table to another, bringing some of them beer, some of them cocktails, some of them Bloody Marys, some of them espresso or water or cola or their checks, washing and drying the glasses and managing the music. Sertac Karan aka Smoky-headed Sertac got up from where he was perched, slipping past the tables and chairs with his empty glass in hand, and, under the watchful eyes of the bartender, took an apron from a hook, tied it round his waist, and set himself to washing and drying glasses without a single word. Sertac Karan aka Civilized Sertac was a housebroken man, trained to do chores, and he stayed there late into the night, past two thirty in the morning, washing and drying dishes and arraying them on their trays. After all the other customers left and the bar was once again empty, and after he paid his own bill—two beers, six tequilas, and an espresso—he said his goodbye to the girl.

She looked back at him bewildered, trying to understand why he had done what he'd done; she took his hands, and spoke to him in an almost-tearful voice. "Is that it then? I'm sorry, I couldn't spend more time with you, there were so many customers, and now if I invite you to my place, you're going to turn me down, I don't know why but I know you will. But anyway, thank you for your help tonight, and I hope to see you again, without the apron, of course."

They smiled at each other.

"Oh! I almost forgot. I didn't tell you my name, did I, and you didn't either. I'm Sabine."

"And I'm Arab," replied Sertac Karan aka Shamilov-number-one-fan Sertac, before walking out of the bar.

Sertac Karan aka Hesitant Sertac had not accepted Sabine's proposal, had not gone to her house, but the girl's ghost wrapped itself around his neck and he would carry her, still clothed, back to his room, and he would make love to Sabine's ghost all night. Sometimes Sabine's silhouette would vanish, her place taken by Dr. Sarîn, or Merasîm, or his first love, or the high-school girl who flashed him, or May, before returning, once again, and finally, to the miserable visage of miserable Merasîm.

* * *

Sertac Karan aka Stayed-out-too-late Sertac was a shameless man, but only in his imagination, in that imagination holding him fast to life but also preventing him from doing things from which there was no return in his narrow room in that dead city.

Sertac Karan aka Wretched Sertac was a deceitful man. "I'm Arab," he'd said to Sabine, and when he suddenly remembered that moment, he burst out laughing. He was drunk; he went and pissed underneath the condom-matic in the darkness, and he let out a fart that sounded like a braying donkey, and then he laughed at the state he was in.

Sertac Karan aka Waiting-for-love Sertac was an avowed man. He kept talking the whole way home, as if he weren't alone, as if an old, old friend were by his side, and as if they had left the bar together. "Sabine, Olga, Tanya . . . they're all the same. No matter how beautiful, how sexy, how alluring they may be, they're not suited to me. The heart wants what the mind cannot bear."

Sertac Karan aka Night-blindness Sertac was a valiant man. At that late hour of the night, he ran into the lunatic nun with the limp as he entered the empty corridor of the guesthouse; as if to ease his fear, she instantly hailed him with a weird greeting. She pointed the tip of her metal cane at him and wheezed out something he could barely hear—"*schlut o flüt u schlut o flüt*" —before hobbling her way to the shared kitchen. *Clomp, clomp, clomp, clomp . . .*

Sertac Karan aka Pill-popping Sertac was a drunk man. In that instant, he couldn't bear to look at the nun's face or at the teeth that made her look like a piranha. Passing by the door of the girl who he still had not yet properly met, he heard the melodies of a familiar song but couldn't discern what song it was or why it so stirred him. Sertac Karan aka Errant Sertac was a drunk man; he entered his room and, still wearing his clothes and his shoes and his bag, threw himself face-first onto the bed.

* * *

It was his fourteenth day in Münster, a Wednesday. He spent it like every other wasted day so far, listening to the German frogs with all the hot-blooded anger of a father. Sertac Karan aka Village-idiot Sertac was already mocking them before he'd even opened his eyes. "Ribbit, ribbbbbbit, suck a dick, you little midgets!"

The morning sun beat down upon his sweating chest through the window, which he always kept open for the cigarette smoke and his bad breath. Sertac Karan aka Sallow-faced Sertac got up and stood in front of the window and looked out; everything was the same as always: the garden, the trees, the bushes, the flowers, the bugs, and the little pond surrounded by lichen-covered stones that housed a chorus of frogs.* They were all pleased as punch, and not just them, but the woman, too, was happy, having cast off her clothes to sun her freckled body on her roof, and her honey-colored breasts, too, were happy. This freedom was her freedom, this country was her country, this body was her body, this home was her home, and the Polish construction workers next door paid no heed to this nude woman as they worked. Before long, she slipped her bikini bottom off her legs and exhibited the fullness of her fulsome freedom to the sun. It was a lovely sight. Sertac Karan aka Getting-out-of-hand Sertac felt like jumping out of his window; he wished he were Superman and could don his cape and fly. But this cape was not his cape, this freedom was not his freedom, nor this country nor this roof nor this city nor this state. It was a lovely sight, but he grappled with

* Frogs have always been a proper menace. They were one of the plagues that God set upon Egypt, alongside floods and lice. Think, too, of the first line that the chorus of frogs croaks at Dionysus in Aristophanes's play: "Brekekekex, ko-ax, ko-ax, / Brekekekex, ko-ax, ko-ax!" As the old Kurdish saying goes, "A frog without its croak would croak." (Trans.)

his own dark thoughts as he stood in front of the window, and so he lit a cigarette—in moments like these, cigarettes were a lifesaver, they really were saving his life, cigarettes were medicine—and Sertac Karan aka Fading-star Sertac longed for his doctor in Amed.

* * *

Ozlem arrived to take him to Frau Müller; the nag was expecting his first piece of writing, which, according to Ozlem, was going to be published in some local newspaper, and the newspaper wanted to interview him. "For which reason," Ozlem said, "you need to dress nicely." Because they were also going to take some pictures of him in the institute's library.

"Okay, fine," said Sertac Karan aka Gold-hearted Sertac, although in truth he was stricken. "But can you please tell me what I should do about the pimple on my nose? Tell Frau Müller that Sertac Karan aka Blood-drained-from-his-face Sertac begs your forgiveness but requests that the interview be delayed by two days, if at all possible. Besides, even if it's not possible to delay, I can't come today anyway. Tell her I haven't finished writing yet, maybe by tomorrow or the next day."

Ozlem mobilized all of her womanly charms to try to change his mind. "It's not a problem, brother Sertac, they can Photoshop your pimple away."

Sertac Karan aka In-a-pickle Sertac glared back with the eyes of a proper Amed lunatic. "And what about my misery? How will they get rid of that? Do you think they can Photoshop away this crushing, lethal misery keeping me from writing no matter how hard I try, Ozlem? Truly, if this Photoshop is such a great thing, then make it do something more for me than just copy and paste! Truly, if it is so great, then make it save me from being colonized, make it let the land I was born in bloom, make it turn my country into a paradise, make it do things even I can't imagine! Make it stop the dirty war, make it bring peace, make it do it all. What's stopping it?"

Ozlem left, ruing the day, and when he was alone again, Sertac Karan aka Pacifist Sertac got himself an empty jar, went out into the garden, and started chasing after the free frogs by the pond.

This story was his story, and he didn't have the heart to finish it.

This story was his story, and it began coiling itself around his dreams.

This story was his story, and it was not without honor, except in his hometown.

As a consequence, Sertac Karan aka Lost-all-hope Sertac beseeched his psychiatrists.

As a consequence, Sertac Karan aka Shattered-mirror Sertac cried out, his voice trembling, "I'm trembling!"

19

EXACTLY THIRTY-THREE days had passed since his arrival in Münster. For exactly thirty-three days, Sertac Karan aka Conformist Sertac had been staying in the *Diakonissenmutterhaus* guesthouse, and according to the plan, he would be spending his final month in a different house, one that was "well-appointed, lacking no comfort, spacious and comfortable and airy, with a stunning view" and, perhaps most beautiful of all, was a "single-family" home. Sertac Karan aka Beyond-his-control Sertac would soon be saved altogether from his guesthouse room and the limping nun who'd lost her mind, and, especially, from the lonely girl who set his heart aflame, even though he'd only ever seen her from afar and, despite all his efforts, had never managed to meet her face-to-face; he'd also be saved from the croaking frogs and the tolling bells, from the long, dingy corridor and from that district and from that street. Sertac Karan aka Balcony-lover Sertac had, over the course of thirty-three days, felt like putting a single bullet in his brain for every single day spent in that guesthouse. He had been locked away and forgotten in some dark prison, his hands and feet bound with the sturdiest of chains and all of his human rights violated; he hadn't wanted to come to Münster in the first place, to settle into that guesthouse, but he had been coerced under threat of force; they demanded a story from him, also under threat of force, and they immiserated him in helplessness, in womanlessness, in uneventfulness, in the silence of the nights, the boundless solitude, the monotonous living, in the deaf country, the yellow color, the inviting repose that held its dominion over these people and these places, in the clouds, in the rain, in everything reminding him he is human, and, especially, in the system of things, that drab and lifeless system, that suffocating system, that oppressive system, that system that proclaims "I am the system," the insatiable system with whose rope, one of these defeated nights, he would hang himself. Whereas the Germans supposed that Sertac Karan aka Miserable Sertac was simply still in a state of shock, having come from the grasp of death to the cradle of life, from hell to Heaven; that Sertac Karan aka Run-ragged Sertac was under the spell of the euros handed to him in a sealed envelope, that he was merely overwhelmed by surprise but flying high, overcome with joy, like some Kurdish bird freed from its cage, utterly astonished by democracy, which he had never seen before, and by freedoms so unbridled that villages in his own country would be razed for even the briefest taste of them. That's why, they supposed, he was so miserable whenever he encountered something interesting; he didn't know what to do with his embarrassment, and after a gulp he would lower his head and continue onward slowly, without any hurry.

* * *

Before the sun set and darkness fell, Sertac Karan aka Bottled-up Sertac stepped out onto the wooden balcony with a bottle of a German wine, Blue Nun Merlot, and sat himself down in a chair directly across from the opposite balcony, where a young German woman was passionately kissing her Italian husband goodbye, and with whose departure she would soon find herself lying underneath another young man, an Easterner, and so he waited with bated breath to watch it all take place.

Her husband would leave the house in the morning with his James Bond briefcase in hand and a swagger in his step, he'd climb into his blue VW Polo with a swagger in his step, and with that very same swagger he'd drive his car out of the open garage door.

He would go to work and she would wait a while on the balcony, sometimes watering the flowers with a red plastic pitcher, and if Sertac Karan aka Most-likely Sertac was on his balcony, she would bobble her head like a bird, greeting him "warmly" and asking him in her perfect English how he was doing, how his writing and everything else was going. And he would reply haltingly with his limited vocabulary. After their brief and awkward exchange of pleasantries, she would take her leave of Sertac Karan aka Flaccid Sertac, and go inside to open the door for her big, brawny young lover. Sertac Karan aka Philandering Sertac could see it all, could see what they did in the kitchen, in the living room, in the bedroom; the woman had purposefully not drawn the curtains all the way shut in her bedroom, so as to let him have his fair share of peeping as they devoured each other—for theirs was not lovemaking.

Sertac Karan aka How-deep Sertac observed their acts of depravity, the trollop bouncing up and down on the man like she was riding a seesaw—which, after all, she was—and sometimes his two hairy hands made their appearance, grabbing her melons and squeezing.

Sertac Karan aka Racing-heart Sertac felt like his brain was melting out of his ears as he imagined the parts of the scene he couldn't see, imagined the devouring and adding to it fantasies of his own, the breathless gestures and godless deeds he couldn't see between the door and the bedroom. The rest of the pleasure was, for him at least, up to the soap in the shower. That was his fair share, after all. "This life of mine," he thought to himself, "without clear beginning or end, ought to be filmed like a *National Geographic* documentary, or, at the very least, I ought to take my place in the same frame as a pack of wild dogs hounding, in their wild cowardice, the majestic lions and tigers. I'm not worthy of Europe, I don't deserve its freedom; the system here isn't to my liking." He was thrilled, nonetheless, to have his fair share of the fun.

That evening, he drank five glasses of wine on an empty stomach. The woman's husband was busy with the grill that night; he lined up sausages and pork chops over the flames. She helped him too, bringing out glasses and plates and spoons and forks and knives and napkins, one by one, onto the balcony, setting the table with meticulous care. Every time she reappeared, she cast a glance at Sertac, narrowing her eyes. She looked at him, at his balcony, at his wine bottle, at his cigarette smoke. Sertac Karan aka European Sertac was in a European city, on the large balcony of a well-appointed house, and there was a woman across from him who slept with an Easterner and caught his Eastern fever, and that very Easterner was now visiting the happy couple at their home that night. He was a guest of the woman and her husband; they all sat on the balcony together, happy as clams. Sertac Karan aka Easterner Sertac stood up with ire, with an ire he reserved especially for Eastern men, and went inside. Besotted on five glasses of wine, the young man's presence defeated him.*

* * *

It was a rainy morning, a pitch-black morning. It was not yet even 9 a.m. by the time Sertac Karan aka Early-to-rise Sertac leapt out of bed. The laptop he kept open and running twenty-four hours a day was on the table, ever so slowly downloading varied and sundry files from a Russian website. The download window hadn't yet reached twenty percent, and Sertac Karan aka In-a-rush Sertac didn't have time; he slapped his hand against the side of the screen and cursed out the computer. He had already complained about the internet connection to that conceited bitch Ozlem a thousand times over, telling her they needed to find a solution as soon as possible, and she contented herself with merely nodding and, ultimately, did nothing at all. He had even told Frau Müller about the problem with the connection. There was, in fact, no problem with the connection; there was merely a download quota, though he was

* Who could help but ache with the *Sorrows of Young Sertac* in this drab and unwelcoming German town? (Trans.)

none the wiser. After hitting the computer, he angrily yanked the plug out of the wall, swearing all the while. His voice was so loud, the harlot next door must have heard him, but he didn't care. Instead, he kept bitching and moaning like a witch with something stuck up her ass, until finally his complaints reached their climax. "Like I even give a fuck!"

He hated weather like this, weather that plunged him out of nowhere into doom and gloom, weather that sent shivers through his whole body. It was not the time for writing poetry. Those beautiful times and lovely days for the writing of poetry had long since passed. Poetry, which once set storms raging, which once reigned sovereign, had fallen into the hands of mindless and idiotic teenagers who wasted their time playing with their phones. Like, who would bleed for poetry today? Who would commit suicide with a poem? The sky broke open bright and early, and Sertac Karan aka Foolhardy Sertac was bare-ass naked. His thoughts were also bare-ass naked as he looked at himself in the mirror, a mirror he'd sometimes take to the bedroom and angle down at the floor, kneeling opposite it so he could look back and see his ass. Sertac Karan aka Prototype Sertac was the author of some truly creative short stories; he would lie himself down on top of women made of pillows, of towels, of ropes and belts, of slippery, soft sofa cushions, and he would go back and forth, slowly... slowly... slowly... and he would rain truly unthinkable swears down on these artificial women from the height of his pleasure, and sometimes he would even look back at the mirror so he could see his balls tighten in their dark sack.

* * *

First, he would shave his head, then he would shave his beard. Then he would iron a pair of pants and a shirt, and he would look high and low for the nail clippers he had lost a few days earlier, but he would not find them, and his frenzied search would cover him in sweat, which would consequently send him into a rage, so he'd take himself out onto the balcony where he would check to see if the dark clouds were skidding away.

For he intended to leave—today, tomorrow at the latest. He needed to leave Münster behind, after sorting and tossing his trash, of course, after a deep clean of the house, after making the bed and folding the linens, after visiting with Ozlem and Frau Müller, after talking to the Easterner; he had things he wanted to tell him, some advice, some questions and suggestions. But he didn't have time.

* * *

"Sorry, brother, I don't mean to keep you."

"It's no problem. I have time."

"True, you do have time."

"Yes, I do."

"So you're a Kurd, from the region of . . ."

"Yes, I'm a Kurd, from the region of . . ."

"My head and my eyes bless you."

"My head and my eyes bless you, my brother, thank you kindly."

"Tea or coffee, or something else?"

"Don't go to the trouble. No tea or coffee, maybe just a glass of water."

"Sparkling or normal?"

"Sparkling would be better, I suppose."

"Right away, brother, sit down, relax!"

An awkward silence.

"You've been in Münster for seven years?"

"Yes, seven years. You?"

"I'm just visiting, been here a month and thirteen days."

"Forgive me for asking, but what work do you do?"

"What do you mean, 'forgive you'? I write stories, I don't know how to do anything else."

"So how do you get by?"

"Royalties from my books, and a few lies."

"I don't understand."

"I'm joking, man! I sell flowers in Amed."

"You sell flowers? Weird."

"What's weird about it?"

"Writing stories, selling flowers? I don't believe you sell flowers."

"When I woke, I saw someone selling flowers."

"What?"

"Nothing . . . It's a line by Seyda."

"Seyda?"

"Seydayê Cegerxwîn."

"If you'll excuse me, I should go."

"Sit down, sit down, there's still time. Water?"

"No, thank you."

"And you? What work do you do?"

"Me?"

"Yes, you. Do you have any kind of job?"

"I'm a caretaker, brother."

"A caretaker?"

"Yes, a caretaker."

"And?"

"And what?"

"And what, or whom, do you take care of?"

"I take care of a disabled kid."

"I see. How much do you make?"

"Four hundred euros a month."

"Four hundred euros? Is that good?"

"It's enough, plus I'm getting a raise soon."

"May God ordain even more for you . . . Do you work somewhere close to here?"

"Yes."

"Water?"

"No! I would like to go."

"Take care of the little runt, then fuck his mom in the cunt."

"What?"

"What do you mean, 'what'? How do you do it?"

"How do I do what?"

"How do you fuck the kid's mom when he's right there? Isn't that a weird fantasy?"

"What are you talking about? What fantasy?"

"You know what I'm talking about . . . So, you're worth four hundred euros?"

"What's it to you what I'm worth? You got something better than that?"

"I'll give you 1,400 euros, right now."

"For what?"

"To fuck me . . . Don't look at me like that, I'm not gay and never in my life have I ever looked at the same sex like that, but think on it anyway—1,400 euros."

"Fuck you and fuck your mom, you dirty bastard, you animal! Just look at yourself!"

"Water?"

"What kind of water?"

"Anise water, an Amed specialty."

"Fuck your sister in the cunt! Have you no shame? How . . . how can you?"

"How can I live with myself? Good question . . . At this point in time, if you ask me, the Kurds can do whatever they want."

"What?"

"We Kurds live not in a postcolonial society, nor in a postmodern society, but in a posthabitable society, you understand me?"

"Take that *post* and shove it up your ass! What the fuck are you talking about?"

"I'm talking about a society that has been torn apart and stitched back together, you fool!"

"You think I need this today? Fuck you, you rotted faggot!"

"Your time is up, I'm well aware; her husband has left the house, go on then, man, be on your way, and say hello from me! Just one last thing: *Fools are those who persist in their mistakes.*"

* * *

This story was his story, and he wished he knew what he was in the middle of writing.

This story was his story, and it was raining.

In that instant, Sertac Karan aka Blown-it-all-up-man Sertac was seeking a deputy minister for foolishness.

In that instant, Sertac Karan aka Yes-indeed Sertac wept at how far he'd fallen.

PART FOUR
Signified

20

BEFORE I INTRODUCE myself, tell you who I am, who my father was, I want to share with you all the details of my life, everything that happened before I ended up right here where I am now, in this cell where I don't know how much longer I'll be staying; I want to tell you about the sequence of events from start to finish, ending with me being thrown into this dingy cell. And, I want to tell you about that teacher. That teacher who everyone made out to be my enemy, except for him alone. Yes, everybody. And so, I want to explain the cause of that enmity, to explain why I first befriended him and then became his murderer. I want to tell you everything; there's still time for everything. He's not here with me himself, not at present. And I don't know when or really how I killed him. But his ghost is so close. His black hair short and dirty as it always was. His big, beautiful eyes sweeter than they ever looked. He hasn't given up a lick of those good looks, which first swept me off my feet. Teacher

Sertac, he always looked practically perfect. Yes, he is here, a ghost, lying motionless on his back. No, I can't reach him, I can't touch him with my hands, I, Alî Osman, I, the only son of Evdilkerîm the Plasterer.

* * *

Over the course of this life of mine barely worth the envy of a dog, I have known very few people—like Mom and Dad, sister and brother, uncle and cousin, woman and money, religion and ideology, leader and guide, and so forth—who have lived, before they fell for something (and I fell), before they depended on someone (and I am dependent), people who have traveled far and wide, have struggled and have stood fast; people who, in other words, have not been defeated, have not succumbed, or who, if they did, managed to recover by means of their perspicacity and their foresight, of their nimble wisdom, and if they didn't succeed in recovering, then like the scorpion of legend they simply put an end to their lives by their own hand, or, as it were, by their own stinger. But that is merely an old wives' tale, biological bluster, for scorpions cannot sting themselves, no, and in any case, stinging themselves has nothing to do with their nobility; anyway, scorpions don't commit suicide in helpless situations—as far as we know. And because they are cold-blooded creatures, they can't bear the warmth of fire—like me right now—so they simply bite the dust. I should tell you now that I, Alî Osman, I, the only son of Evdilkerîm the Plasterer—the plaster he mixed stuck to every wall but the walls of my mind, for reasons that are not clear to me—I am not a scorpion nor am I in any way like a scorpion. But

I have known scorpions, have understood them, have come to know what they are and what they want from me, how dangerous they are and how potent their poison is. I know of their treachery, of their portentousness, of their carelessness. I, Alî Osman, I, the only son of Evdilkerîm the Plasterer, I know them well. I know I have nobody now to lean on; I am all alone, abandoned, orphaned, and like my father I have a mouth and no tongue and I am helpless and cowardly. Like the voice of the terrible man who threw me into this ring of fire from behind that iron door said just moments ago, my tongue will manage to speak on its own, my mouth will need no force to open up, and I will begin confessing. They will make me sing, as they said, like a nightingale, so come on then, *cheep cheep cheep cheep cheep cheep* . . . This fear of mine keeps my lips sealed; these things my tongue doesn't know how to speak, these secrets wet under my tongue, one by one they will all come to light. One by one.

For a few days now, here, the scorpions have been able to reach me, even though I'm in this pitch-dark cell, and they could sting me in an instant; to them, this is mere child's play, and they are certainly not children. So many of them are just like me. They never meant to get into this shit; they were in the spring of their lives when they sank into this quagmire. I saw it, I heard it: So many people who left their houses in the morning and never came home, so many people left without fathers, without brothers, a vast majority of them executed point-blank with a single bullet to the back of the neck on some street, or in some teahouse, or in some store, or in some field, or in some room, or in some well, or in some hole, or else on the bank of some serene river or on the side of a highway far away from the city or near some shrine or in some graveyard or in their car, or else otherwise they were found strangled, with the rope still around their necks. And I, Alî Osman, I, the only son of Evdilkerîm the Plasterer, I bristle at death, especially a death as terrible as that, the same as I bristle at scorpions, at their tails and at their segments, at their saturnine silence, at their sudden strikes, at their souls and their beards, at their clacking prayer beads and at their eyes, above all their eyes, at how they lay their eyes on me and it feels like my soul is being ripped from my body and I am petrified. The scorpions I've seen, the scorpions in teahouses, in shops, in houses, they would approach me and talk to me for hours, would threaten and intimidate me with violence, would force me to kiss the Holy Qur'an *mwah mwah* dozens of times and bring it to my brow dozens of times, would insist that I pledge to give up on my dangerous and oppositional views and opinions, that I not oppose them even if I do not support them, that I follow the true path, that I strive for God and for Prophet and for Them above all else, that I begin to pray, that I go with them to mosques, that I participate in the Community of Faith, that I make visits with them to religious foundations and guilds, that I rid myself of all obstacles that might prevent me from becoming a fully devout believer, that I embark first with my family, beginning with my parents and then, no questions asked, onto my sisters who walk around uncovered and with fingernails polished, that I transmit the message of God to the impure and the makruh, to those who have strayed from the path, that I know my friends and know my enemies, that I distribute pamphlets and deliver greetings, that I stay away from certain people and devote myself to knowledge, and I said to them, "I can't do it, I'm not cut out for this kind of thing." And I added, "I swear, I will keep praying, I will follow the path of God, I swear; just don't make me kill Teacher Sertac." But they were insistent, and they didn't stop following me, deep into the night.

* * *

There was a time when I was surer of myself, of my lifestyle, of my beliefs and my thoughts, of my actions and behaviors in society, and, most importantly, of my mind and of my words, and I am proud that I considered myself in those days, which seem so far from me now, to be the kind of person who is aware of everything. Sure, I was not so dear to most of my friends, but most of them liked me; Mullah Îdrîs liked me. I would leave the house and make my way to his bookstore at the end of the market, and as soon as he saw me he would stand up from his ancient stool and give me a wink and greet me with deep respect and reverence, with both my hands in his, with so much warmth it was perhaps a little exaggerated, and he would ask how I was doing, how my family was doing, and what I was doing at university—he kept up with it all. And then he would seat me in his "boss chair"—he got a little upset when I called it that—and would sit himself down on another stool and begin speaking, drawing me into some intense dispute. The Mullah had quite clearly not opened this narrow, tiny, single-roomed store to support his family; it always struck me more as a meeting place, a gathering point, and not just me, many other young people went there. Our good old Mullah Îdrîs would put his skill in the art of oratory on full display for us, speaking and speaking and speaking with a heavy, deep voice that none of us could believe came out of his tiny body.

That Friday morning, when I left home for school, I changed my mind on the way and went down to the market instead, hoping to ask Mullah Îdrîs a few questions. But I had apparently come too early; the shop still hadn't opened. A few people in the teahouse next door had gathered around the newly lit stove, rolling their cigarettes and smoking, so I went in there to warm up—the weather was cold and my jacket was too light—and have myself a tea as I waited for our guy. All the people inside looked at me, and I gave them a very sincere greeting in return and sat down before I ordered a tea myself.

* * *

The topic was "me," or rather, it was my thoughts and the impression I gave of bookish leftism, and when I embellished my words with a few lines from Nazim Hîkmet, Mullah Îdrîs was undaunted, looking at me with affection as he said, "I've told you before, so let me say it again, Nazim was a good poet, I've read so many of his poems, but the issue isn't Nazim's poetry. Set that aside for a second and tell me, why do you ascribe certain events to fate and fortune, and why others to nature? What kind of contradiction is that?" He brought up uncertainty, my uncertainties, followed right after by Islam, its actually existing form, and he brought up faith and the individual, the individual and philosophy, philosophy and atheism, atheism and Marxism and its shortcomings, Plato and Aristotle and Descartes and Leibniz and Farabî, before finally he brought the topic around to Teacher Sertac.

* * *

They say your capacity to think is directly proportional to the size of the place where you live; in other words, however expansive a place is, that's how much your thoughts expand, advance, spread in all directions, and however narrow a place is, that's how narrow your mind and your heart become; you have no way of seeing either yourself or your surroundings, as a consequence of which your mind adjusts itself to the scale of the space it occupies, and you end up seeing the things you do as totally singular accomplishments, totally unique and unmatched in the world. But no, they are not, truly they are not, the way a door that closes on its own does not know it holds someone captive.

* * *

Sure, I didn't pray, I didn't fast, I didn't go to mosque or to lodges or to sermons. I paid no heed to my teachers' recommendations or advice. What drew my attention at school wasn't Arabic or Tafsir or Hadith or Fiqh or Kalam or the Holy Qur'an or History of Religion or History of Islam or Recitation, but calligraphy, Husn-î Xet, which was being taught not by the proper teacher of the subject but by Teacher Sertac, the tall, dark, and handsome Kurd who had been teaching classes at our school for two years, Teacher Sertac, who was warmhearted and kind and wise and astute. I really liked him and the strange methods of teaching he used. In fact, among the students I don't think there was anyone else who stood up for or supported him as much as I did, which is perhaps why he was reproached as a sinner; sure, I was a sinner myself, and according to the rumors spread by some simpletons, I was an idolater against God and the Prophet, a nonbeliever damned to eternity in the flames of hell. And so my befriending Teacher Sertac would harm him, and indeed it did him as much harm as it could. Because in the end, he was merely earning his daily bread, and so I was devastated when I heard he had requested a reappointment and would be leaving the school and everything else behind.

* * *

One morning, we saw that Teacher Sertac had parked one of those old shabby trucks at his house and was moving. I was on my way to school with a few friends. We wanted to help him, to lift some of those sacks filled with his belongings, but he disapproved. "No need," he said, a little angrily, as he went and stood beside his pregnant wife. In a state of shock, we continued walking. Because that day we were supposed to work on a few examples of Aqlem-î Sitte, the so-called *Six Pens* of Arabic calligraphy, but it wasn't meant to be, especially not for him.

* * *

Where were we? I was telling you about Husn-î Xet; perhaps it was only because of how fine my handwriting is that my teachers with their cropped pants and their sweaty foreheads didn't bother me more. They believed my mind was being sullied by the communist agitations of Teacher Sertac. Under normal circumstances, this problem would have been resolved with time and by God's hand. And yet as the days passed, the world began feeling narrower and narrower to me. I would try to expand it, to get myself a little room to breathe, by opening my Husn-î Xet notebook filled with examples and abstracts and articles and notes, and I would read page after page. More than half of this notebook was scribbled all over with the Esma-u'l Husna—the *Beautiful Names of God*—and in addition to that notebook, I had another notebook that I certainly would never have brought to school. Almost all of its pages were embellished with nearly every style of calligraphy by Sheikh Hamdullah of Amasî, like Sûlûs and Nesîh and Rikaa and Tewqî and Reyhanî, and I couldn't get enough of looking at them. I had also filled a section of the notebook—maybe twenty pages—with doodles in the Kûfî script; not for nothing, because Kûfî, also known as Ma'qil-î Qelema and Xetê Setrencîlî, was composed of straight, rigid lines, hard angles, and subdued, simple geometry, and so it was simpler and easier to write; and yet, whenever I tried to write in Kûfî my pen would slip, my hand and my fingers would surprise me with their betrayal of Kûfî, leading me to round its corners, bend its bars, loop its ligatures, shear its sharpness; and suddenly, I sensed that what guided my hand in this way, what caused me to glide my pen in these curved and looping shapes was nothing other than my heart itself, and I understood I could never accept imprisonment; I would always and ever want to live free.

* * *

So I killed him.

Unfinished Endnotes

1 Yes, okay, fine, but why are you asking me? Hm? Why did *I* make him blow a gasket? No, it's not a metaphor, he really did blow a gasket, threw it across the room, pelted it through the air till it smashed into that picture of my dad, may he rest in peace, leaving it with neither frame nor glass. As if I had anything to do with him going crazy, as though I wanted deep down to see him lose his marbles; never mind how he started writing all about our lives, goddamn it, fucking with our livelihoods no less, poisoning our lives with his venom, not only shoving that poison in my face like it's my fucking fault but then, on top of it all, turning everything into this shit show!

2 What did you say? Huh? Why did I leave him? Why couldn't I make do? Yes, yes, you're absolutely right, nobody loses their shit without reason, they have to have a reason! Psychological or sociological, concerned or unconcerned, you think I'm the real reason, don't you? Whenever men lose their way in

upside-down societies like ours, the justification is always a woman, or several. Do I really need to speak at length about why that's ass-backward? You all know what's been going on, what happened to us. You don't even have to go far: Start with yourselves, for instance, just look at yourselves and the lives you deem proper, and proceed from there as far as you can take it. But please, for once, listen to me, just once, that's all I ask. I'm saying this not because my home fell apart, or because I became, in essence, a widow, overwhelmed by the hateful glares of those fixated on my lack of honor. I certainly don't pity myself or my situation. The weird thing is, despite everything, I feel bad for the state he's ended up in. I don't even understand why I feel sad, or why I cry whenever I think of him. I know as sure as my name he won't marry anyone else after me, he won't be able to have any kind of intimacy with other women, none at all. I know him better than any of you, and knowing him for so long has left me frozen, closed off, to everything, everything, everything! No, I can't hear your voice. I tell myself that instead of marrying a writer who spends twenty-four hours of the day whistling, I wish I'd married a drunk, a miscreant, a lazy sack of shit, a blind cripple; if nothing else, then I'd have something to say to his venerable friends who've suddenly lost their voices, who've squirreled themselves away in the holes of who knows whose mothers, sisters, and wives!

3 He woke up as usual at the ass crack of dawn, but not because he had to piss. This time it was because of that rancid goddamn anise water. It was supposed to cool him off inside, supposed to cleanse his internal organs. After three shots, he

was supposed to have been saved from all his troubles. Wasn't the philosophy of that baneful liquid based—in large part—on the notion of "inner purity"? Just like that whole business of catharsis—what a good comparison, God, between catharsis and anise water! As Aristotle writes of catharsis in his *Poetics*: "The task of tragedy is to effect, through fear and pity, the proper purgation of these emotions." It must have been with this in mind that he had poured not one, not two, but three shots of anise water on the offal soup his mother had made, filled with oil and sumac, descending into hell in the evening and falling asleep early, without getting to work on liberating his country, so he wouldn't be sleepy the following morning. He couldn't remember quite when he had fallen asleep, but when he woke up with a stomachache and jolted up in bed, he made like lightning for the toilet. In that window of time, unable to control himself—of course he had no control over it—he let out a few squirts in his underwear. His ass muscles hadn't been able to hold back the leak, and a rancid smell filled the air. Tragedy struck: He had shit himself. His dirty underwear in one hand, a green bar of soap in the other, he scrubbed and scrubbed. The strangest part of that midnight chaos, in that bathroom filled with the traces of every fluid, were the words pouring from the crooked mouth of Aristotle: "The task of tragedy is to effect, through fear and pity, the proper purgation of these emotions." Catharsis by anise water, or, put differently, the tears of a man, scrubbing shit-covered underwear, whose sleep and whose night had been abysmal. His greatest fear was that his mother might descend upon him. Strange, the woman who could never sleep because of his dad's farts hadn't awoken in those terrifying minutes, and he emerged from the bathroom wearing wet underwear to make his way back to hell, his own private hell. He went back and forth between hell and the shitter until dawn broke, because his stomach kept making fun of him.

4 The house was his father's house even though the deed was in his mother's name, and Sertac felt neither safe nor sound there. He was under surveillance; the two of them wanted to see what he would do, how he would spend his time, whom he would see, and what he would read. They had the power and, as Foucault says: "Power is everywhere." Power, in other words, didn't operate solely in the marketplaces, nor solely in the teahouses, the schools, the prisons, the hospitals, and the workplaces; power had penetrated all the way into the city's brothels, into its market in bodies. The goddamned war, the civil war between oppressors and oppressed, had sprung up, had entered into their homes, their rooms, even their dreams. Sertac was afraid; he was suspicious, which was why he scrutinized his parents like he was a spy. As soon as they sat down to dinner, he stealthily observed his mom, his dad, his older brother, and his sister, Canan. He knew the tea placed in front of him wasn't poisoned—the poison of choice would be rat poison, of course—yet still, just in case, he waited for them to take a sip first before he followed suit.

5 She had four gigantic cats—Sertac thought all four of them were faggots—to catch mice, by the apparent grace of God, and they were fed a steady diet, every meal liver or boiled

meat, even while the street cats had to eat one another's snot, they were so hungry. Catching mice, yeah right. After eating, they tiptoed their way to the wool beds she had gotten for them, curled up in the corner, and spent hours licking their assholes and balls and tails and necks and taints and stomachs before drifting into deep sleep. People would ask how those faggot cats were doing, instead of asking after Sertac. If one of them coughed weird they would rush the poor pussycat to the veterinarian, but whenever Sertac fell sick they didn't give two shits. He couldn't say why, but as soon as any of them crossed paths with him, they would turn away and click their tongues, as if chiding his depravity.

6 Yes, he had quit smoking cigarettes for a while, for a few brief hours in the evening, at least, but this decision absolutely wrecked him at night. He practically lost his mind. Together with Mihemed from Lîcê, on one hot summer evening—his wife, Merasîm, hadn't been home since noon; she had gone to a friend's place to stay the night, or rather, they had gotten into a fight that Friday morning, they started by bickering until Merasîm began flinging whatever she could get her hands on at Sertac's head; apparently they had entered the kitchen to make themselves a lovely little breakfast, he was working, the wife was watching TV, the situation began over a few eggs and lots of food, but soon escalated into an outrageous brawl—they were grilling on the balcony, gobbling down morsels of meat as soon as they were cooked, without feeling the need to slide them onto skewers, and they shot the shit as they sipped furtively on their glasses of araq. Somehow

the topic turned to how to properly light and smoke the single shitty cigar they were currently sharing, and, taking his turn to smoke, Mihemed explained to Sertac the trick to properly smoking a cigar. “See, this is how you have to take the drag, long and slow,” even as he himself struggled against the coughs tearing through his throat. It must’ve come out of Teacher Sertac’s mouth. “Good Lord, cuz, we need to quit that shit!” And his friend latched on to Sertac’s wrist; they tousled playfully for a second until they made a bet—they vowed to each other then and there to toss their packs into the fire; in fact, they even took a picture to mark the occasion, the moment they’d quit smoking cigarettes, and after their revelry came to a premature and cigarette-free end and his friend left, Teacher Sertac finished the remaining araq, swilling shots from the bottle without any water or food so that he’d fall asleep fast, but this only made things worse and worse. He was craving nicotine, and the craving engulfed his brain whole. It was so bad, he felt like biting into his own flesh. Like some amateur burglar, he began turning over drawers and cabinets and boxes and pockets and bags and suitcases and trash cans and every last nook and cranny in his house, looking everywhere in the hope that he might find an unfinished cigarette or even just a cigarette butt. He truly looked everywhere, between books, in his shoe rack, in the bathroom trash can and in the trash cans outside the building, but his efforts yielded no fruit. Nor was there anyone nearby whom he could go and ask. He had moved in here three weeks earlier and still hadn’t managed to connect the telephone, even though he had gone to the post office four or five times since he first applied to ask what the holdup was. His house was also off the beaten path, standing alone in an empty field; the marketplace was in the pits of hell, and at any rate he had no intention of going there at night, plus he might not even find an open store if he did. Not to mention he feared the police like he feared nothing else. Right as he thought about the full-body search they'd conduct on him, he became nauseous and dragged himself with great difficulty to the bathroom. He couldn't remember when or how he fell asleep. He awoke in some late-afternoon hour the following day and, without even washing his face, ran in his slippers to the market. So had gone his quest to quit smoking, and, right now, he wanted to roll a cigarette to go with a strong cup of Nescafé.

7 Right then my dad showed up. He was still standing in the threshold when he started swearing with his gruff voice, keen to talk about what bothered him that day, and, of course, he had to bring up the people of Amed again, directing his rage in particular at the village women who kept him from coming home with a couple kilos of eggplants. "They wake up bright and early so they can stampede to the market and fight over the eggplants, grab as many as they can get their hands on. Who cares how many kilos, like psychos!" And on he went. "What the fuck kind of people are they? Why do they love eggplant so much? What on Earth do they do with so many vegetables? Babakanooch or some shit like that, the motherfuckers!" And he would distort his mouth to mimic the accents of the eggplant

eaters. "Wallah we ganna eat us sum babakanoooooch. Wat? Wat? Babakanooch! Wat? Babakanooch! Eat a dick!" And he grabbed the tip of his dick and came in without even taking off his shoes, handing the bag of eggplants to my mom. "I got eggplant for you right here, woman!" And then he headed right back out to the market. He had gone, he had left, but in that instant my whole world came down around me, everything went dark, I don't even know what happened to me. (from Sertac's notes)

8 What did I say just now? I had only used the words "eggplant" and "stroke" in the same sentence. That must mean they added something to what I wrote and passed the page off to my father in the evening. He came back, beat me with whatever he got his hands on, God forgive him, and then he trapped me in the bathroom. I was naked, bound and gagged, and the water was freezing; I was shivering, and my mom slapped me so hard, it turned my ears red, those very ears she filled with the wails of her weeping. Mom might have been sobbing, but I couldn't hear her properly. Why, Dad? Why, for God's sake? Was I always like this? Was I always sick in the head like this? Didn't I used to be your one and only son? You would get me cookies and toys and ice cream and candy and balloons. When I was little, Dad, you took me to your barber and held my hand tight so I wouldn't be afraid of the buzzing clippers. Do you remember too, some bright, clear night, Mom went to draw water from the well in the courtyard of the mosque across from our house and the bucket got caught on something in

the well, so you tied one end of a rope around your waist and the other end around the windlass of the well and you descended into those pitch-black and terrifying depths, and I did not stop sobbing until you emerged again? And since that night, whenever I encounter a well, whether in a book or a poem or a song, whenever I even see the word "well," well, I feel crazy. I thought you killed yourself and I thought you did it because you were disappointed in me... That's why, Dad... Dad, do you remember—yet another painful memory!—one of those first nights after the September 12 coup, a few soldiers raided our house; our eyes were wide as saucers watching them, and they searched the house for anything having to do with us being Kurdish, and when they didn't find shit they left, cursing and swearing all the while. Yes, Dad, I thought you'd get out of bed that night and kick them, attack them. But you were overcome with trembling, and in that horrible darkness the beads of sweat amassing on your forehead shone something wild. And do you remember, when you took me to that swimming hole, the one where the water was always muddy—it was full of snakes and frogs and crabs—and we swam together, or rather, you took a couple of strokes out while I clung to your back? Has it really gone by so quickly, Dad, all that time when you suffocated me with your love? Has it really vanished so quickly, all of your fatherly adoration? Whenever I smell tobacco, I think you must be near. But when you abandoned us and went off to that shithole of a village, you didn't ask after us for months, and I couldn't stop crying.

9 No, no, I couldn't believe it. But the drooling half-wit who was her first love, her boyfriend before me, had given her a book by Ümit Yaşar Oğuzcan* and inscribed it with giant, clumsy letters: "You'll regret it." So, were these the times he had in mind? Anyway, I never would have believed that I could one day break my beloved's heart, that I could so devastate the person closest to me in the world, the person who stood by me even despite all my mistakes, all my idiocy and my foolishness, my heartlessness, my sins and my transgressions and my fornications, all my nonsense that I paid no heed to because I thought it would all eventually resolve on its own, and I certainly never would have expected her to fly into a rage so quickly over such vacuous things, such tiny little problems, reasons so paltry they wouldn't fill the shell of a walnut. I destroyed this home of ours with my own two hands, I see that now. I never deserved her love, but it's too late now, it's over, we've separated. So let her "mom" and her "dad" take a victory lap right up their wrinkled asses, let them dance in celebration in that rat's nest they call a home. As for you, Mother and Father: You never got much good out of having a son like me, and you never will! From the first day you never loved me, and I alone know what havoc you wrought upon that poor woman, and upon me after she left! I curse that day and I curse you! That day I invited the girl to your rat's nest and that doe-eyed creature, ten years younger but a hundred times smarter than me, entered into your home—excuse me, your rat's nest—and I presented

* Honestly a pretty middling mid-century Turkish poet, really only read, as Sertac suggests, by "drooling half-wits." (Trans.)

my youthful beloved before your dour visages, and fearfully announced the entrance of "my blushing bride." And I ate shit, really and truly I ate shit for thinking you human. "No matter what happens," I had thought to myself, "they're your mom and dad, you need to show them respect; pay no heed to whatever they may say, and be sure not to bite off their heads in response." And still I wondered, "Maybe they don't like my doe-eyed darling, it's possible—but who would they have liked, except for my dad's stuck-up niece?— they might not have liked her, they might not have liked that she's headstrong in her own special way, and smokes cigarettes in front of men, especially men like my father, or maybe they simply didn't jibe to begin with. But, ultimately, for my sake, they mustn't say something awful or embarrass me." Yes, that's reasonable enough, I said to myself, and yet you ended up saying what you wanted to say right to her face. First you, "Father," and then you, "Mother," you beat me like tyrants that day, completely without pity, which is why I cut ties with you entirely, and which is why the situation has only gotten worse as time goes on. (from Sertac's notes)

10 Time was short for him to apply to *The Competition of Unfinished Stories*, and Merasîm was on pins and needles; she kept intruding on Sertac's hermitage with anxious, childish excitement, wanting him to hurry up and finish the story the way she wanted it to end. She demanded he "give up" his work as soon as possible. "Or else," she would say, this "profligate wife" to her useless husband, "or else you'll never lay eyes on it again, you can be sure of that!" In other words,

given what had only just recently happened between them, Sertac Karan aka Rankled Sertac would have to spend another week or two kissing her ass, and it would surely be the death of him. Merasîm, meanwhile, imagined herself counting out with her own two hands the thirty thousand lira in cold, hard cash that the center had offered up as prize money; she was so sure of her own suggestions to her husband, indeed of his "pen"—despite the fact that he wasn't one of those writers who "had" "books" "published"—that a devilish smile spread across her face as she talked about the banknotes, speaking to him with both hope and mockery. "C'mon, you bastard, why else would you spend all that money on books and journals? You've already squandered half our marriage on those wasted ambitions, dumping whole loads of money on books *in Kurdish*, for God's sake, so what now? What good's it done you?" She was right, in a way, she had a point. He hadn't gained a single thing from reading or from books. His friends who spent every summer traveling with their families to the paradisiacal beaches of the "country" and who spent ten, maybe fifteen days having the time of their lives in Bodrum, in Antalya, in Olympos, and in Marmarîs, home to Kenan Evren, the junta's head honcho—they'd wear cheap trunks and bikinis as they swam, for free, in the deep blue sea, and then they'd come back to these ill-fated lands filled with joy, with kindness, with unbridled mirth, showing off their bronzed faces and smiling under their mustaches. "Look at you, Sertaco, you read so many books! God bless, you've got the right idea as always, what business do we Kurds have going on holiday anyway?"

And Sertac Karan aka Nonconformist Sertac would have no idea how to respond, so he'd remain silent, unable to decide what he should do, whether he should regret not going or staying or else spending all his money at the beginning of every month on those good-for-nothing books. Then he'd say, "Take off those dirty glasses so I can look into your eyes." And they'd take off their sunglasses with tremendous and painstaking hubris, and where their eyes were supposed to be Sertac Karan aka Flabbergasted Sertac would see nothing but two pitch-black holes. He'd lose his mind, the color would leave his face, and right then he'd hear Merasîm's voice. "Sertac! Sertac!" And he'd jolt awake and call right out for his mother. "Mama! Mama!"

11 Now, too, Merasîm and the story competition alike became a nightmare for him. The missus would leave home every morning and go to her job at the nonprofit, the *Association for the Rescue and Rehabilitation of Dreams That Are Dead in the Water*, which was, as the broad pink sign outside proclaimed in big white letters, "open twenty-four hours," and she'd toil over documents and petitions, and she'd bicker for no reason with her brand-new airhead of a secretary until seven in the evening, which is when she returned home and sat down to dinner to tell Sertac everything, cursing the poor secretary with the most unthinkable vulgarities. "Soot-pussied bitch! You think you know me? You have no idea what I could do to you. Just wait till I shove a donkey dick up in you, then you'll see. Get fucked, you whore! You mongrel cunt!" In moments like these, Sertac Karan aka Cowardly

Sertac seldom found the bravery to look Merasîm in the eyes; he'd avert his gaze, lowering his already-lowered head even lower—he didn't want to be party to the matter—and think of other things, asking her neither about her work nor why she came home late. Besides, in these modern times, are there men brave enough to ask their working wives—their partners!—such mundane things? Where might those fearless and valiant heroes be found, who might they be, where might they live? This world was a woman's world these days. Unfortunately, that's how things were now; women were everywhere, they were many and they were multiplying, they were on the minibuses and regular buses, they were in the markets and at the shops and on the avenues and in the squares. They were standing in the doorways of hospitals, as if maybe they were sick. But really, were they sick? Sertac didn't believe it, he didn't believe they were sick. If they were really sick, then how could they stand on the front lines of every demonstration and uprising in the city? If they were really sick, would they make themselves targets for the cruel cops and their brutal truncheons? What about the men, the men of the city—men like Sertac? What were they doing? They offered their so-called solidarity to their wives, leaving when things came to blows and ensconcing themselves in their teahouses. Which meant then it was not just truncheon beatings, but revolution, yes, revolution, that belonged to women, those unmarried women, those women without headscarves, those ululating women who wanted freedom, as if modernity hadn't given them enough; they were now using all the sophistries of postmodernity to attack their husbands. That's exactly what Merasîm was doing. "But," Sertac said to himself, "Merasîm is not one of those women with a wandering eye, nor is she a proper housewife." She was, however, bad-tempered. She could prattle on and on like there was no tomorrow, would not entertain even the slightest insinuation that she pipe down, and was always looking for a reason to fight. It was like she yearned to take hold of ashtrays or vases or glasses and crash them down on the other person's head. He pitied himself as he went on thinking, "I ought to write a book on being a pussy-whipped pushover, as a lesson for future generations." And he thought about how exemplary he was in this regard. He thought and thought, thought about Merasîm's beauty, about her charms, about her winsome coquetry, and her dizzying scent, for Merasîm was like a blushing bride, a virgin behind her veil. But in bed she was a firecracker; she fucked like a fatherless whore, like a cave made of flames to swallow him alive, like a prostitute learned in every last detail of the carnal art of lovemaking, though in those moments when she was overcome, she'd cast aside all her scholasticism and begin to moan. "If not for your thing, Sertaco, I'd have long since . . ." She'd have long since left Sertac, except in those days the little lady was fixated on his storytelling; not the storytelling itself, but the cash amount of the prize, which as soon as she heard about it—three months ago now—she demanded that Sertac write a fine story. "I've earned that thirty thousand, why let it go to some skid mark of a writer?" There was so much else she said, and now every night she'd sit down with her paper and her pen and her calculator and come up with crazy projects and outrageous plans for that thirty thousand, which, it must be noted, they had yet to win. "Thirty thousand is not a small amount of money, Sertac, have you or your father ever seen thirty thousand as a lump sum? Well, you're going to, you bastard! Thirty thousand, just think about it, thirty thousand, that's thirty times your monthly salary. I'm going to count out each and every one of those crisp new banknotes while you watch. God is great, Sertaco. We'll go to Bodrum, we'll go swimming in the sea, for do we not have a right to get a tan? First, I'll get these hairs taken care of. You ever heard of laser epilation before? Hmm? Maybe I'll get a nose job too, by God, I'll do it!" Sertac Karan aka Like-hell-you-will Sertac thought to himself, "I had your back just for you to sink your dagger into mine, you conniving bitch! I'm going to write that story and then, and then I'm . . ."

12 Fretting over the "story" part of his short story, Sertac Karan aka Storyteller Sertac couldn't make any headway. How could he now, with his homelife in disarray? What could he do to mollify his wife? What, what? He hadn't the slightest idea. He didn't even know if it was daytime or nighttime. He had slipped out of bed silent as a serpent in order to keep from waking Merasîm and gone into his jackoffice, occupied as it was not only by the desk and black leather chair that his father had given him but also by so many other things that it had effectively become a de facto storage closet, and, for hours and hours, he sat there waiting for inspiration to strike, without writing a thing. Could you force your way

into being a writer? With threats, with coercion? Shouldn't writing come freely? Shouldn't he have a say in how it goes? Mustn't a writer refuse to sell out? Wasn't that, after all, the right and ethical thing to do? Never mind for thirty thousand, even a hundred thirty thousand, right? And as if that weren't enough, the missus was forcing on him her shameful ultimatum. "Steal! If you're not gonna write, then steal!" In his confounded state, Sertac Karan aka Absorbed Sertac contemplated his books; he contemplated their publication years and their covers, the format of their printing, their relative condition. No matter how many times some of them had been read, they still looked clean and comely, as if they were hot off the presses, never yet touched, never yet opened. But some of them had, as books are wont to have, fingerprints and tea and coffee and snot stains and pen and pencil marks. Merasîm didn't care. She didn't give a shit about any of it, she would just cross her legs and ask him how the story was going. Sertac Karan aka Ready-set Sertac would reply without hesitation, "I'm still writing, it's almost done." This story was his story, and it was unfinished.

13 "In some places, you make the story run into dead ends; for example, the attitudes of teachers and the cruelty they inflict on students, in my opinion it's not worth bringing up November 10 here. Sure, November 10, the day of Ataturk's death, serves here as an allegory. It could even be that the incident is true to life, but it doesn't quite fit; in this state it reads like a collage of vignettes. Instead, it might be better if you discussed the life of one of the teachers and proceeded

like that, in order to delve deeper into the topic. As for the fig tree, good, you need a tree here. I had a mulberry tree in mind, but you said fig instead. Fine, then; if nothing else, the fig is an ancient and mythic tree. They say its leaves were exchanged as valuable gifts in ancient Greece. It also connotes fertility, which, you already talked about children and their reproduction. That's all good so far. The cultural significance of the fig is also an important point, a symbol of pure morality, but I don't want to dwell on it at length right now, because aside from the fig's mythological meanings, it's also used as a religious and cultural symbol to such a degree that we'll really open up a can of worms if we think about it too much. But, at any rate, I liked the images in Sertac's three discoveries: lying, masturbation, fear. Three subjects that actually have a lot to do with one another, although if you look at the story in terms of its plot development there's no clear connection among the three; in other words, Sertac wants to get in the shower and masturbate in peace, and so he lies to his mother. His goal isn't to get clean; to the contrary, he takes the bar of soap directly into his hand without a single thought about what it means to be dirty or what he might feel after he ejaculates, and here of course the soap calls to mind the concept of cleanliness. In other words, Sertac is engaged in an act of dirtiness with an implement of cleanliness. But also, is masturbation not, in the end, itself a kind of lie? For if we get to the heart of the matter, the Sertac in the story is lying not just to his mother, but to his body as he tries to conjure in his mind the images of women's breasts, closing his eyes so that they'll look as close as possible to the real thing as he rubs one out. In a way, he is lying to his body, know what I mean? And I believe this because my Sertac, the Sertac Karan who is my husband, also lies to his body from time to time, and I don't understand why it is that married men would do such a thing. Why live with women when you get so much pleasure from touching yourselves? You deceive women with your romantic lies to marry us, and you ruin our lives exactly as you ruin your own lives. No, I really don't get it. Why would my Sertac take a shower before making love to me?

"But *neyse*,* how did we end up here? No, don't shake your head at me, don't be embarrassed by what I said. I'm speaking the truth. If it's a lie, then say so. You have a mouth and a tongue, don't you? And thank God for that! For instance, even though we have never, ever made love, and even though I have been far from the warmth of a man for a very long time—far but not free, at least—I have never lied to my body and I never would lie to my body under any circumstances, and I do not share your opinion on this matter and I would never agonize over such things the way you do.

"But *neyse*, please take the masturbation scenes out of the story and stop leading your story back there all the time. I don't want you putting such inane things in a story woven

* "Neyse," Turkish for "anyway," is a dismissive filler word that also means "whatever." It appears twenty-five times in the Turkish translation of the Bible, and not once in the Turkish translation of the Qur'an. Curious, huh? Anyway, whatever. (Trans.)

by a woman. They'd never award me the prize for that reason alone. I know those kinds of people, and yet, on the other hand, Sertaco, dear, you have exactly ten days, you've got it, you've got it, you'll finish the story in those ten days, because if you don't, then goodbye and good riddance, fuck right off. Ten days isn't much, you know, so do what you have to do, but when your ten days are up, you're going to deliver me a complete dossier, understand? If I win first prize, just imagine, Sertaco, visualize it in your mind, if I win first prize and come home victorious, so long as they don't pull a fast one and give it to one of their cronies, I swear on my mother's life that I will send you to Heaven with pleasure every single night, and I'll get you off thirty thousand times before that thirty thousand is spent, understand? Why the pouty lips? I'm not kidding—you and the story you write and me and every night, what more could you hope for?

"But *neyse*—this word is getting on my nerves now!—but *neyse*, Sertaco, give the story a beautiful title, make sure it's super poetic. Remember how you wrote poetry once upon a time? Remember, Sertaco, how you seduced me with a poem? Do you still have it memorized? Course you don't... I do, but I don't want to recite it now, since we've pulled away from each other... What I mean is, you're good with poetry, so give it a poetic title. Why have we pulled away from each other? For what reason did our love fall short, Sertaco? Why did it crash and burn? Why did it go down the drain? Why did we fall to pieces, Sertaco? Surely you haven't fallen for someone else? Hmmmm? No? Then why? I don't believe you'd do something so horrible to me, nor I you, and I don't believe you'd do something so horrible to yourself, so what do you have to say? You never say anything, Sertaco. You're silent, always silent, never any response. Ugh, your silence, my God, your unresponsiveness! It's only with me you don't speak up. You're only silent with me. As soon as the topic of us and our relationship comes up, your voice goes out the window, not a trace of it to be found anywhere. Why is that, Sertaco? Why is there no trace of it? How come you won't look me in the face? Is there another face more beautiful than mine, Sertaco? Eyes more beautiful than mine, Sertaco? Sertac the Revolutionary? More like Sertac the Sterile! No trace of your revolutionary self left either, is there? I thought you were going to liberate a nation. I thought you were going to free a people from their bondage. What happened? Hmmmm, what happened? What are you looking at, Sertaco? At the corner of the couch? At the blank wall, at the window, at the curtains, at the cover of the book on the side table, at the buttons on the TV, at your fingertips? You look at everything except me. Don't you think that's strange? Oh God, I'm done for, oh God! Woe is me!

"But *neyse*, Sertaco, cat got your tongue? Ten days, I tell you... Tie a ribbon round your finger so you don't forget, understood? Coming back to the story, I think the **EVET** brand of oil isn't bad, as an image. Obviously, it's the Turkish word for "yes," but you should have added something more, like how **EVET** oil was super popular in those days, how familiar the logo on the can was, and you could have made the image richer by embellishing it with the jingle; then that part would have been stronger. You don't remember it? Grab your pen and write, quickly!

"Köyde, kırda, dört bir yanda,
Bereketli sofralarda,
Yağınız var mı?
Evet! Evet!
İştah açar mı? Evet! Evet!
Çorba, güveç, baklava, börek,
Güzel yemek, sağlık demek,
Hem nefistir hem de leziz,
Evet yağı çok sağlıklı,
Hem çok hafif hem hesaplı,
Üç öğün de Evet! Evet!
*Sen de kullan Evet! Evet!**

"Oil, Sertaco, oil! Makes you think right away of the phrase 'burning the midnight oil,' doesn't it? Because in those dark and scarce times, who among us could get their hands on beqlawe or borek, no matter how much they worked? Was there really any 'bounty' or 'mirth' to our meals in those

* In the village, in the country, all round the Earth
At tables full of bounty, full of mirth,
Do you have oil?
Evet! Evet!
Did you work up an appetite? *Evet! Evet!*
Beqlawe, borek, soup, and stew,
Good food is good for you,
Not just yummy and delicious,
Evet oil's so nutritious,
Tastes both delicate and ambitious,
Three meals a day with *Evet! Evet!*
Do yourself good with *Evet! Evet!*

days? If there was, why couldn't we taste it? Yes, pretend doctor, yes, I'm shocked, how could you forget it? But now you're pondering and pondering: How is it that a woman like me could dig up something so deeply buried in the ground of this unfinished story?

"But *neyse*, Sertaco, let's get back to the **EVET** oil, which means yes, which means saying yes to the system, yes to oppression, to poverty, to abject misery, yes to the fascist regime. **EVET** means yes to corruption, yes to greed, cowardice, and subjection, and I could keep going, Sertaco. If I wanted, I could find so much more underneath it, but that's enough already, Sertaco. Apart from a few small and occasional mistakes, I don't think there's a problem here we can't solve. To tell the truth, I'm stuck on the image of the hideout, your hideout on the roof; you talked about your school uniform and the fear it stirred in you, and I think you could have delved a little deeper into the relationship you had with the hideout. It would be better that way. The hideout was destroyed after the soldiers came, for example, which, all right, but what was life like in Zerdav before that destruction? That point needs to be illuminated. It doesn't have to be detailed, but you really ought to add some sections on life before the soldiers, right? Don't you think? And the school too; yes, sure, it was an ideological state apparatus, as Althusser would say—it still is, to be honest—but you must be wondering how me and Althusser crossed paths? How many years have we been married now, Sertaco, and you still don't know me? You still think I'm a complete nincompoop, but *neyse*, let's put a pin in that topic for now. We'll come back to it later.

"Please take the name Merasîm out of the story. I don't want you to use my name. Whaddya say? The romance between Sertac in the story and the cop's daughter is interesting. If you had loved me that much, I'd have done anything for you! Hand to God, I wouldn't have left you wanting for anything at all. Am I a jealous person, Sertaco? I don't care what shit you did with anyone before me, but as for me, I tasted of love with you. There's nothing before you and nothing after you, no, no, God as my witness, I'll never leave you; if I really, truly, sincerely wanted to leave you, I'd have done it a long time ago. I'd be so ashamed before my family, my relatives, my friends, and my colleagues, I'd have no idea what to say to them. This is all to say, Sertaco, that I'm not afraid of you, I just never came to really know you. I always considered myself a good judge of character, but that's over with too, thanks to you; after so many years, my Sertac forsook himself, no, he shit the bed, so take my name out of the story, my name which appeared to you in a dream has no place in your life. Take it out, I don't want it, buddy, take my name out of there!

"But *neyse*, Sertaco, the girl leaves the Sertac in the story and his whole world turns yellow, but Zerdav, where is Zerdav? Does such a place exist in Kurdistan? No! Another symbol, another defense mechanism, another attempt at obfuscation. Why? You need to clean that up too.

"And then, the corpses of the guerrillas in the courtyard of the municipal building, those scenes, those images are so, so important, Sertaco. You used the same image in one of your earlier stories, if I'm not mistaken; as I recall, you showed it to one of your novelist friends for feedback and editing. Not an issue. The words of the people of Zerdav are important too, of course; you've handled them well, showing that there are also stupid people in this imaginary Zerdav, for instance, but *neyse*, it was a good call to cut the commander's words short—more than enough nasty, mean words in that scene, like 'terrorist,' 'Armenian,' 'hoodlum,' 'cum stain.' I don't know how much of that was made up or not, but leave them for now, don't change a thing.

"When the girl leaves, the Sertac in the story experiences a yellow autumn, a 'jaundiced autumn.' The phrase is so poetic all on its own, a really powerful line, beautifully done. I liked that whole section. No need to change it, in other words. Apart from that, I want to say to my Sertac, I really like Pîra NAH; I like how she confronts Sertac every so often in the story, how she makes the occasional appearance, although we know so little about her, like all we know is that she's some witchy hag. We don't know who she is or where she's from or why she's haunting the Sertac in the story, but it works well there. Her presence doesn't trouble us as readers the way it troubles the Sertac in the story, so just note that in your mind, got it?

"But *neyse*, thank God Pîra NAH isn't a very clear character. In fact, it's her obscurity, her otherworldliness, that suits her to the story. I might say Pîra NAH is a kind of relationship: the relationship that the Sertac in the story has with fate, a relationship with his own fate. I don't know what kinds of meanings you had in mind, but that's how she seems to me. You used Pîra NAH like some kind of sinister owl, but you've also figured her as a piranha. I get it, you're making a play on words, but it's here, right here, that I see an additional relationship: the one between **EVET** and Pîra NAH, which is to say the relationship between "yes" and "no"; and when you put both of those names side by side, they open up the story to a completely different reading altogether. My God, Sertaco, you are crafty!

"But *neyse*, Sertaco, I'm not saying this to flatter you. Let's deflate that big head of yours, which you've already injured twice, and bring you down to Earth. Listen to me, the posters of the movies you watched as a kid must've left an impression on your brain, right? That's no doubt how you came up with Pîra NAH, don't you think? See, this is why I'm saying I never really came to know you, I truly haven't known you at all, but now, thanks to all these comments, every last thing in that subconscious of yours is coming to light, bit by bit. The situation with Xelîlko, his dad, and the bookstore—I felt so bad for Xelîlko there, not for the Sertac in the story, no. Do you know what image I had in mind when I read that? Xelîlko, a boy, ten to twelve years old, right? A gaunt, swarthy little kid, he looks like a plucked bird. His tiny heart races, fluttering almost, the color draining from his face as he approaches the Sertac in the story. His face is covered in scrapes old and new. His hair has been shaved clumsily, almost even angrily, with clippers that were probably broken; its mortal scars on his skull are visible, the beatings have left him mentally unstable, he's always drooling, always smiling. Yes, this is the kind of person he is, poor Xelîlko. Like I said, I felt so bad, my heart broke for him. And the words that Xelîlko's father had for the Sertac in the story, especially the part where he dissects Sertac's personality with that weird philosophical dichotomy and accuses him of ignorance. You might not agree, but I feel like I saw some hesitation there, the writer hesitated, I mean; the Sertac in the story doesn't give the necessary response to his friend who has in an instant become his enemy. Out of fear? Because he's afraid? Perhaps out of respect? Or out of ignorance? He wants to say, 'There's no ego more disgusting than your ego!' But he doesn't—he wants to say so much more, but he doesn't make a sound, he just rushes out of the shop, and as soon as he does, he begins crying without knowing who or what on Earth those tears are for. Are problems solved by crying? If they were, Sertaco, then would we have ended up as we are? But *neyse*, Sertaco, I think you get my point, and now I feel a headache coming on. But before I finish what I have to say, I have another suggestion about the situation with Codename Revolution and the Lower Quarter, about the holy water from Zamzam, about the hate that the Sertac in the story has for his paternal uncle and his dimwit wife, about his maternal uncle Mihemed and the black combat boots, about hope and about death. But I guess that can all wait until tomorrow, all right? I've worn myself out, Sertaco. I want to sleep now; I'm going to lay my head down and fall asleep, without you."

14 Sertac had been listening with undivided attention and care to his darling Merasîm, the "critic," until that very moment, when her last words sent shivers down his spine and he leapt from his seat and glared at her. "What did you say?"

he commanded, his eyes wide as he gulped once or twice, and indeed he was right, she *was* talking about Pîra NAH making an appearance in his story, and Merasîm couldn't stop talking about her. The plot necessitated that Pîra NAH would have to appear every so often, but he was sure as his name was Sertac that he hadn't been saved from the police, that he hadn't made mention of Pîra NAH's arrivals or her departures, neither in the story nor anywhere else. This only served to deepen his fear; his body was overtaken by a cold sweat, and a strange shiver seized hold of him. It all happened before Merasîm's very eyes. She stood stock-still, not so much as a hair moving on her head; she merely watched him and laughed—she laughed and laughed until Sertac fainted altogether.

15 The heart reflected in the eyes . . . Before noon they took me to the cave. I understood what was going on once I saw them coming into the Big Room at night, in and out, in and out. "Go to sleep, now," was all they said to me. No, I didn't sleep. It's not that I wasn't sleepy, or that I was losing sleep over something. But still . . . in the morning, I would see my face in the broken mirror; the two bright-red hollows of my eyes would scare me sometimes, and so to keep from having an altercation with the mirror, I'd rush out of the bathroom. I would stay up most nights, my sleep piss-poor, and when it did come, half the time it was plagued by nightmares, and the rest of the time it was filled with crazy dreams. As had happened for the past three nights, that night was spent half standing, half sitting, and found its end as I read and

memorized poems by Rojen Barnas. I'd look at the still-made, untouched bed. Ah, sleep! Sleep, you daughter of an infidel! You are so close and yet so far! "Go to sleep, now." What a sweet phrase. She spoke in an admonishing but nonetheless soft tone, and she smiled too. She smiled. I said to myself, "Come and ask me about it, Gulperî, and by the way, doesn't your name mean 'rose fairy'? Rose fairy, fairy of roses, none but I know the sorrow of sleeplessness, none but I . . ." No, there was no need for a meeting; I needed to go.

"There's a long road before you."

The blonde-haired, green-eyed tarot reader had said so. "A long and dangerous road, filled with things that could strike at any moment."

And the candle on the table went out all on its own, without her blowing it out. Everyone waiting there fixed their eyes on me, and I felt like they were watching my cruel fate play itself out. I saw the pity in their eyes. In the end, I was seeing her for the second time in my dream. It was an intense and nasty dream. She used those seventy-eight tarot cards to slice paper cuts all over my body, and she pressed salt by the fistful into all my wounds. Filled with fear, I slammed my fist into the comrade next to me. "Misto! Misto! Wake up, please!" The guy was in a deep and contented sleep, letting out a crazy snore, and there was no waking him. Only I was awake. In the morning, they knocked on my door and came in: Ciwan, Lewend, Gulçîn, and, of course, Gulperî. She went as she always did right to the window, swinging both panes wide open to purge the acrid stench of cigarettes. A fresh coolness filled the room. "Tobacco smuggler," she joked.

"You did a number on those cigarettes again. Clearly you didn't sleep." Apparently, I hadn't slept. After opening the window and yawning happily at the day, she sat in the chair next to me, and the rest of them began yawning. It was a strange scene.

16 In the beginning, I was, like every light Kurd in this land, hard and horny: proud beyond measure, arrogant beyond precedent, pretty irritable and dissatisfied with everything except myself. Like every modern Kurd, market days were a source of joy for me; waking up late after a restful night of sleep, I'd make my way to the shower, whistling all the while. It was my custom, taking a lifestyle magazine from the newspaper rack next to the toilet, to read as I did my business. I had recently put a radio in the bathroom. Like every sophisticated Kurd, I adored classical music, especially Paganini's "La Campanella." You would think it wasn't just my suds-filled ears listening but the fragrant soap, which washed over my body in gentle concord with the music. It was nourishment for the soul, music, and I sated my soul every single day. Like every good Kurd, I asked the porter to pop out and quickly pick up two loaves of bread fresh from the bakery—still warm if possible—and a couple of the day's newspapers. I prepared my breakfast with a strange meticulousness: two soft-boiled eggs; little bowls filled with various jams; braided cheeses that looked like a girl's pigtails; herbed cheese; qaşar cheese; honey and butter; clotted cream and heavy cream; a dish of yogurt; three kinds of olives, Çelebî, Domat, and Edremît; roasted peppers; Nutella; sausages

and cold cuts; a bowl filled to the brim with bananas and oranges and apples and tangerines, quinces, and kiwis; and roasted meats. After arraying my table with it all, I'd turn on the TV and, before I sat down, I'd make myself a coffee, around which time the bread and the newspapers would arrive, and like every conscientious Kurd, I'd first read the latest column from Mîne G. Kirikkanat. What the good woman was talking about that day, whom she was lambasting, which side she was feuding with, whose business she was throwing a wrench into; like every loyal and truehearted Kurd, I would read whatever that troublesome woman had written before moving on to the other columns. In the beginning, I was patriotic, like every Kurd; I had the porter buy me a single Kurdish-language newspaper so he'd run my errands more quickly and wouldn't suspect me of anything. Whenever I wrote anything, I displayed the tendency to start every word that began with the letter *v* with a *w* instead, sometimes accidentally making the ones that start with *w* start with *v* instead; for instance, "verb" turned into "werb," while "writing" evolved into "vriting." Once, I remember, a friend asked me what the Kurdish word was for "period," I mean for "menstruation," and I translated it verbatim from the Turkish, *aybaşı*, into Kurdish, "month head." I told my friend, and he used that completely meaningless phrase in an article that went on to be published in a magazine. Things got so bad that whenever my Turkish friends encountered a Kurdish word, they wouldn't call anyone else but me to find out what it meant, and like every disconnected-from-reality Kurd, I came up with ridiculous translations for them. In the beginning, I was blind like every Kurd. I couldn't see the gem hidden in all words, their deep and rich meanings, every last one, no matter how much I examined them. No, I couldn't understand what they meant or why they mattered, couldn't grasp what the big deal was, which meant that, like every literate Kurd, in the beginning I was also mistaken and I had taken the wrong path through this life. Merasîm? She left, abandoned me. I mean, how, like, how should I explain from the very beginning who I am and how I ended up teaching at that school? Why? Okay, fine, you ask your questions here, now. Yes, it's true, I don't believe in your God. I still don't. No, I'm not a communist, I'm not a leftist, I'm not devout either. So how did I end up at the Imam Hatip School, you ask? Well, that's just how things turned out.

About Sandorf Passage

SANDORF PASSAGE publishes work that creates a prismatic perspective on what it means to live in a globalized world. It is a home to writing inspired by both conflict zones and the dangers of complacency. All Sandorf Passage titles share in common how the biggest and most important ideas are best explored in the most personal and intimate of spaces.